THE
LOST CONTINENT

Atlantis is a legend that has refused to die. The ancient Egyptians told stories of a fabulous island kingdom that sank mysteriously into the sea. Plato spoke of a utopian paradise located beyond the Pillars of Hercules. Edgar Cayce revealed tantalizing glimpses of Atlantean society and predicted the amazing discoveries off Bimini. Now Martin Ebon explores the secret of Atlantis, tracing the latest evidence from Thera to Crete to the Yucatan peninsula to Bimini and the Sargasso Sea, following the trail of a legend, a people, a culture, and a place that long ago vanished from the surface of the earth but left behind a mystery and a memory that still puzzles the mind of man.

ATLANTIS:
The New Evidence

ATLANTIS:
The New Evidence

by
Martin Ebon

A SIGNET BOOK
NEW AMERICAN LIBRARY
TIMES MIRROR

ACKNOWLEDGMENTS

The author gratefully acknowledges the cooperation, advice, and guidance received from individuals and organizations in the preparation of this volume. Foremost among these were William R. Akins, Dr. Maxine Asher, Michael Ballantine, Chariklia E. Baltazzi, Brett Bolton, Wanda Sue Childress, Anne E. Cusack, Panayotis Martakis, Dr. James W. Mavor, Jr., Dr. William Niederland, Egerton Sykes, and Dr. David D. Zink. Among organizations and agencies which provided help in research for this book were the Association for Research and Enlightenment, the Greek National Tourist Office, the Ancient Mediterranean Research Organization, the German Archaeological Institutes in Athens and Rome, the Greek Ministry of Culture and Science, and the Athens Archaeological Society. The author, alone, is responsible for facts and conclusions presented on the following pages.

Contents

CHAPTER 1

Atop the Volcano

Beneath this sea lies the secret of the legendary sunken island-continent of Atlantis. I write these words on the very rim of the volcano that forms the island of Santorini, surrounded by the waters of the Aegean Sea in the Eastern Mediterranean. Leaning over the rocks that separate the upper roadway from the steep cliffs of volcanic rock, I look down into the bay which is actually a water-filled volcano itself, deep and dark. And in the midst of this bay of Santorini, guarded now in early morning mist, lie two forbidding-looking volcanic islands which, as geological time goes, rose only quite recently out of the sea. Sulfurous fumes still emanate from them, for they are not quiescent; they are a direct link between the vast disruptive force within the earth, and all of us who live precariously on this planet's shell.

We fear volcanoes, and we are right. Our short memories can insulate us from the potential dangers beneath us, but only as long as we chose to ignore the hot, bubbling reality below. I once stayed overnight inside the rim of an extinct volcano, Mount Kintamani, on the island of Bali. A twelve-bed hotel had been built in it. The volcano had long ago been tamed; memories of the last disaster, in the 1920s, had faded, and I slept without disturbing dreams. But Santorini is different: the turbulent past, which spans at least 3,500 years of massive upheavals, is ever with us. The series of volcanic eruptions on Santorini (also known as Thera) were so severe that it now seems certain they caused the destruction of an advanced civilization which the ancient Greek philosopher-poet Plato called Atlantis.

Just when and in what time sequence this legendary Atlantis was destroyed is of little consequence as we look down into the seemingly bottomless bay, the "caldera" (which shares linguistic roots with "cauldron") that is partly encir-

1

cled by Santorini and the smaller islands that form this group. This is stark, brooding, dark reality—in vivid contrast to the bright and cheerful wall paintings that archaeologists have found underneath the volcanic dust that covers this island.

Since Plato spoke of Atlantis, much speculation on the island's or continent's life and location has come our way. Were the Atlanteans capable of technological feats that rivaled or exceeded our own? Are we—or some of us—reincarnated former residents of Atlantis? Was there sufficient warning before Atlantis was engulfed, to enable its inhabitants to escape and take their arts and sciences to other parts of the world, ranging from Egypt to the Americas? And was Atlantis, as its name implies, situated in the Atlantic Ocean?

We will try to answer these questions later on. Right now, atop this volcano, we are facing reality, not legend, not imaginative thoughts or ingenious combinations of scattered facts that might suggest one or another answer to the Atlantis riddle. The new evidence that has emerged, and which promises to give the most definitive replies to questions about Atlantis, is right here, within the caldera in front of us and on the archaeological site of Akrotiri, right on Santorini itself.

These rocky rims of the island-volcano are in themselves concrete evidence. One look at them, and you see varied layers of red, gray, black, brown, and white; explosions from the very innards of the earth have caused this palette of colors. Cinders, slag, lava, and above all pumice have settled, one on top of the other. You see them first from the boat as you arrive at one of the two small harbors—Thera, also known as Fira, and Athinios. They stand out clearly, one level discernible above the other, each representing a long period of the island's volcanic history.

While the caldera is too deep for boats to anchor, small craft visit the concrete and visible elements of the island group's violent past: the Palaea Kaimeni ("Old Burned Island") and Nea Kaimeni ("New Burned Island") that squat inside the bay. A trip to Nea Kaimeni, which appeared within the caldera in the early eighteenth century, leads us to the island's Bay of Petroulion. It is a steep walk up to the island's peak; there is no shelter, and the climb is hot and exhausting.

Being arduous, the climb gives plenty of reason to stop and look around. Lava and volcanic ash are now and then interspersed with small patches of vegetation that, with nature's persistent daring, pop up among the otherwise barren hillside. Here, too, are layers that suggest the islet's intermittent growth since it emerged from the sea in 1707; ravines, cuts in the surface, and indentations in the ground are geological evidence of growth.

By the time we reach the peak of Nea Kaimeni, there can be no doubt that this is the very rim of the volcano. We are looking straight down into its King George I Crater. Erratically escaping sulfur fumes remind us that here we have a glimpse of the earth in its most unsettled essence. To anyone, this is an awesome sight that needs no reminder of Santorini's destructive history; the sense of violent drama, past and future, is all-pervasive.

But how does the existence of the Santorini volcano link modern science with ancient Atlantis?

It shows concretely that, in prehistoric times, this volcano within the Aegean Sea experienced an explosion for which there is no known parallel in extent of violence and potential damage far beyond its horizon. Supplementary evidence comes from excavations which began in 1967 on Santorini itself, in the village of Akrotiri. These excavations have demonstrated that the island was a lively, culturally advanced part of the Minoan civilization, of which the Palace of Knossos—on Crete, south of here—is the most widely known example.

Under the direction of Professor Spyridon Marinatos, who died in an accident within the excavation site in 1973, Akrotiri has yielded works of art, tools, housing structures and other elements of civilization that place its cultural role firmly within Minoan life. Marinatos advanced the hypothesis that the outbreak on Santorini caused such flooding of Crete's shores that whole segments of its seaside were destroyed; at the same time, outpourings from the volcano must have rained ash and pumice onto Crete in such quantity and density as to bury Minoan civilization, including the Palace of Knossos, and to drive out the inhabitants.

Just what the chronology of these cataclysms was, or whether Santorini (Thera) itself was the actual Atlantis Plato had in mind, no one can tell for sure. Archaeologists, geologists, volcanologists, and a new breed of scientists—submarine archaeologists, can marshal many facts to support different views. The whole science of dating items found in excavations is still relatively young, and specialists argue about specifics in their learned journals. The matter becomes still more complicated when you find remnants of civilizations that have been submerged by the sea for centuries or millennia; water, sand, and tidal forces make dating extremely difficult, and erosion beneath the sea creates different patterns than it does above ground.

If Santorini's vast eruption about 1500 B.C. is at the core of the Atlantis idea, what about reports of Atlantean remnants elsewhere? After all, some authorities maintain that Atlantis was an actual continent within the Atlantic Ocean, with such islands as the Azores mere remnants of it. Also, quite recently, undersea expeditions in the Caribbean, near Bimini, have pointed to a submerged civilization; evidence linked with Atlantis has been reported off the coasts of Spain and Ireland, in the North Sea, and elsewhere.

We need not discourage current and future explorations beneath the seas when we assume that—at this particular time—the new evidence on Santorini is probably the most persuasive of all presently available data linked to Plato's texts. What makes this evidence persuasive is the very nature of the Akrotiri excavations; here we can measure on-the-scene evidence against academic controversies and colorful but thinly documented claims.

I walked through the Akrotiri excavations about a decade after they had begun. What Marinatos and his colleagues unearthed was a town sufficiently accessible—that is, not too deeply covered by volcanic rubble—so that modern techniques and tools could preserve it as fully as possible. While the delicately colored and designed frescoes (wall paintings or murals) are now on display at the Archaeological Museum in Athens, the Akrotiri settlement is clearly visible as a series of houses, streets, craft centers, and storage facilities. There is virtually no doubt that the people who lived here about 1500 B.C. were first driven from their dwellings by a disturbance that may have been a strong earthquake; later, the volcanic explosion covered the settlement with debris.

The Atlantis controversy must be considered in the light of modern archaeology, its achievements and its limits. Three names now stand out in discoveries that are milestones on the road leading us back to ancient Greece. One is Heinrich Schliemann, of whom we shall speak in a later chapter and who discovered Troy and Mycenae; the other is Sir Arthur Evans, who unearthed and reconstructed the Palace of Knossos on Crete and coined the term "Minoan civilization"; the third was Marinatos, who first drew attention to the presence of pumice in the Cretan village of Amnissos—which he attributed to volcanic emanations from Santorini. Spyridon Marinatos published the results of this archaeological detective work in a paper, "On the Legend of Atlantis," in the scholarly journal *Creta Chronica* in 1950; the full text of his paper forms an appendix to this book. World War II had interrupted his work. Marinatos and his colleagues engaged in other excavations during the immediate postwar period. But once they began the Akrotiri diggings, they got results fast, and in large number.

One can walk through a museum and become quickly numbed by vase upon vase, figurine upon figurine, statue upon statue. The virtue of observing an excavation such as Akrotiri lies in the intrinsic quality of its layout: this, indeed, is where people lived their daily lives, some 3,500 years ago; the products of their imagination and skill are clearly visible. Putting the work of Crete's Minoan artists side by side with those of Akrotiri, the unity of style becomes obvious in the delicacy of images of flowers, women, animals—blue monkeys jauntily moving from branch to branch, for example—as well as in subject matter and materials used.

Marinatos, reporting on the 1969 season of excavations, stated that it was highly unlikely that an eruption such as that on Santorini could have left Crete untouched. "It is impossible," he wrote, "to ignore the catastrophic power of the tsunamis," the destructively high and strong waves that would have hit the Cretan coast. He added: "It is impossible, therefore, to imagine that Crete and other places in the Eastern Aegean escaped terrific damages by the tsunamis around 1500 B.C." This, of course, suggests that the search for Plato's Atlantis does not end on Crete, nor on Santorini nor anywhere else. It opens up totally new avenues to the imaginative and energetic scientist.

The magic name "Atlantis" provides powerful impetus to fresh ventures into the human past. When French marine explorer Jacques Cousteau brought his boat *Calypso* into the Aegean Sea, he not only explored the area around Santorini and Crete, but made a special underwater search of a little island, Dia, north of Crete and in the direction of Santorini. No doubt, a wide public can learn from Cousteau films that the search for lost civilizations should extend to further areas beneath the sea. Particularly the shelves extending from land areas and islands into the waters of the Aegean and elsewhere could yield valuable material that might mesh with the new evidence that has now been found.

All this, or at least much of this, might not have happened without Plato's words about sunken Atlantis. Because his descriptions were preserved, we have been given a term and an image that stands for much more than yet another ancient artifact brought to light by a shovel or a diver's retrieving rod; Plato gave us a vision of what we once were and might once more become.

CHAPTER 2

The Echoes of Plato

"Before Plato: silence; after, echoes." This is how Hans Schindler Bellamy summarized the role of the ancient Athenian poet-philosopher in his book *The Atlantis Myth*. Schindler is representative of scholarly belief that no verifiable sources concerning Atlantis preceded Plato. He writes: "Altogether about a hundred Atlantis references are found in the post-Platonic classical literature, but they add no new aspects or facets to the great philosopher's myth."

Atlantis began with Plato, and we who seek proof of its existence and ponder its fate and meaning are his heirs. But who, in fact, was this man whose head we only know from awesome sculptures which may or may not be faithful replicas of his appearance? What was the world in which he lived, that provided the framework for his life and work, which nurtured but repelled him, and which made him yearn for—and write about—a utopian society that would be radically different from the anarchic Athens he knew all too well. Quite aside from Plato's description of Atlantis, there is a fascination within the man himself with a society quite in contrast with the pattern of life he saw around him. It was a period when democratic ideals had become debased by excesses. The fourth century before the birth of Christ, not only in ancient Athens but in many other city-states and communities in the Eastern Mediterranean, was one in which chaos and tyranny were engaged in one of the cyclical struggles that has been part of man's recorded existence—then, before, and after.

The political ideas Plato expressed in his major work, the *Republic* have often been described as being utopian. This term suggests that Plato envisioned the ideal state; yet, looking back, Plato's form of government would have contained elements of ruthlessness quite intolerable to our contemporary outlook. The Atlantis he pictured was a different reality, or a different vision—although one may regard the Republic and Atlantis as contrasting sides of the same philosophic-political coin. But, above all, we must see Plato and his visions as products of his time and place. And what, precisely, were they?

The drachma had fallen to a new low, the army which had been sent to Sicily had been defeated, the excesses of unbridled democracy were everywhere to be seen, and the government was falling. These were not matters, however, which seemed to concern any but the patrician classes; like the slaves for the average men who thronged the streets of fifth-century Athens, these were matters over which they had no control.

To describe the streets of ancient Athens would be to catalogue all the conditions of man within Athenian society. Here, you would find wretched beggars squatting in the dust, peddlers singing their songs, slaves upon some master's errand, workers waiting to be hired for the day, the scribe offering to write your letters, the stranger seeking a bed for the night, tradesmen and shoppers haggling over prices—and, perhaps, despite the din and confusion, one might have observed Plato walking and quietly debating with one of his young disciples, much as his master Socrates had done many years before.

Such bustling groups of people would have left, inevitably, unimaginable litter. Plato must have taken the mud and refuse of the streets for granted. The accumulation of broken pots, crumbled mud bricks, and household garbage, combined with road dust, must have made a quagmire every time it rained. The stench in summer can have been little more pleasant. To understand the conditions under which Plato lived, we must forget all of our modern notions of comfort and sanitation and be prepared to be impressed when an excavator solemnly reports the discovery of one primitive drain.

In the *Republic*, Plato himself gives us a brief picture of everyday life under the restored democracy: "The horses and asses have a way of marching along with all the rights and dignities of freemen; and they will run at anybody they meet in the street if he does not leave the road clear for them; and all things are just ready to burst with liberty."

Plato (427–347 B.C.) was one of the greatest prose writers, and perhaps poetic epigrammatists, of Greek literature, as well as the most influential of Greek philosophers. While it may be an exaggeration that all of Western philosophy "constitutes but a footnote to Plato," nearly all of the major themes of Western philosophy were first sounded by Plato. Most of his thoughts were expressed in the form of dialogues, of which the earlier are vivacious and distinguished by an almost fictional use of characterization, most memorably that of Socrates. In his later works, his style grows more expository, a dramatic shift which tends to confirm his identification with Plato (Platon), the poet whose birth dates (429–347 B.C.), were almost those of Plato the philosopher, and who was also a disciple of Socrates. If they were the same man, Plato's *Phaedrus* and *Symposium* may provide us with the spiritual link between the amatory epigrams and the philosophical books. Certainly, as nearly exact contemporaries and disciples of Socrates, the two men, if indeed they were not the same man, must have known one another. Perhaps another confirmation of their identity may be found in the *Republic*, his most famous work, in which the ideal state is set forth, allowing for the Atlantis writings, and the problem of social justice is worked out in the fullest detail. In that work occurs Plato's condemnation of poets, in which he excludes them from participation in the government and even from citizenship. One might see in this writing the opinion of an old man who had been a poet in his youth and knew well what socially unreliable types and troublemakers they are.

Still other causes for the dictatorial state Plato presents in the *Republic* and, to a lesser extent, in the Atlantis writings, lie with the unhappiness in Greece following the defeat in Sicily, the position of Plato's family in the social structure, and the ravages of unbridled democracy he had seen in his youth. An aristocrat, he and his family, friends, and followers regarded the existing constitution with suspicious discontent. His writings retained the high-minded idealism of youth, his refuge in a political Utopia was doubtless influenced by the disgust he felt in a self-indulgent democracy.

Still other influences on his political and social philosophy would have been his own poetic efforts (which we know him to have made, although he may not be the Plato whose poems have survived), his attraction to Cratylus, the Heraclitean philosopher, and later to Socrates.

Socrates was the deepest and most lasting influence on

Plato's life, but we must assume that a youth so educated and eager for knowledge was also informed about the other philosophers in Athens's age of decline. We must assume with Benjamin Jowett that it is unlikely Plato "should have made no attempt until his thirtieth year to inform himself as to the achievements of the earlier philosophers, should have learned nothing from his friend Euclid about Eleatics, nor from Simmias and Cebes about Philolaus: that he should have inquired no further respecting the doctrines continually brought to the surface by the public lectures and disputations of the Sophists, and left unread the writing of Anaxagoras, so easily obtained in Athens."

During the trial of his master Socrates, Plato was absent, claiming illness. However, many of the aristocratic young disciples of Socrates made similar excuses. It is possible that Plato was also being cautious about associating himself with his former teacher. Accused by the tyrants of Athens of "corrupting the youth," Socrates may indeed have been guilty, but the "corruption" would have been homosexuality rather than philosophy. After the death of Socrates, Plato and other disciples went to the city of Megara, there to study with Euclid. Tradition has it that Plato also visited Egypt, where he acquired his knowledge of Atlantis, to Cyrene, Magna Graecia, and Sicily. This exile, or journey, consumed some 10 or 12 years, and it seems clear that Plato studied with the Italian Pythagoreans, whose mathematical knowledge he mastered. In Sicily, he visited the court of Dionysius the Elder, and caused offense by his plain speech. For his moralizing, he was turned over to the Spartan ambassador Pollis and put up for sale on the slave market. He was returned to Athens after being ransomed by a Cyrenian philosopher, Anniceris.

After his exile from Athens, Plato appears to have first seriously set himself forth as a teacher, following the example of Socrates. According to the testimony of Aristotle and other of his pupils, Plato seems to have taught with a combination of discourse and dialogue, to have shared a communal life with his students, and rarely to have accepted payment in the form of presents. His overriding desire seems to have been not to be a statesman himself but to form statesmen, to set forth ideals which would regulate actions.

Upon the death of Dionysius the Elder, his son invited Plato to Syracuse. Plato accepted, hoping to win over a reigning king to his philosophy, but the young man soon wearied of Plato's seriousness and grew jealous of his relationship with another statesman, Dion, whom he banished. Plato returned again to Athens, presumably a sadder but wiser man.

His later years have been well described by his most famous English translator, Benjamin Jowett: "After some years, at the renewed solicitations of the tyrant and entreaties of friends, he resolved upon yet another voyage to Sicily. His immediate aim was doubtless to attempt a reconciliation between Dion and Dionysius; to this may have linked themselves more distantly, new political hopes; the undertaking, however, turned out so unfortunately that Plato was even in considerable danger from the mistrust of the passionate prince, and only evaded it by the intervention of Pythagoreans, who were then at the head of the Tarentine state. Whether, after his return, he approved of Dion's hostile aggression toward Dionysius, we do not know; but for his own part, from this time, having now attained his seventieth year, he seems to have renounced all active involvement with politics. The activity of his intellect, however, continued amidst the reverence of his countrymen and foreigners, unabated till his death, which, after a happy and peaceful old age, is said to have overtaken him at a wedding feast."

Upon his death, *Critias*, and therewith our most complete record of Atlantis, was left unfinished, thereby adding to our tantalization. There appears to be only one reference to Atlantis prior to Plato. In his commentary on Plato's *Timaeus*, the philosopher Proclus says that the historian Marcellus wrote, in his now lost *History of Ethiopia*, that "the inhabitants of several islands in the Atlantic Ocean preserved a tradition from their ancestors of the prodigiously great island of Atlantis which was sacred to Poseidon and held dominion over all the islands in the Atlantic for a long period." Thomas Taylor, in his translation of *Timaeus*, quotes the following reference of Marcellus to Atlantis: "For they relate that in their time there were seven islands in the Atlantic Sea, sacred to Proserpine; and besides these, there were others of an immense magnitude; one of which was sacred to Pluto, another to Ammon, and another, which is the middle of these, and is of a thousand stadia, to Neptune." However, Proclus says nothing regarding Marcellus's sources; one presumes the islands to which he makes reference are the Canaries and the Azores.

Considering the enormous appeal of Atlantis to the imagination of subsequent generations, the lack of earlier references does appear strange. The reason is usually, and most conveniently, laid to a loss of documents. One version of Plato's knowledge of Atlantis is the Solon, the wisest of the Seven Wise Men, learned of the myth in Egypt and intended to revive its acceptance 150 years before Plato, but political difficulties prevented him. And as Plato repeatedly emphasized, the memory of Atlantis disappeared among the Greeks because those who knew of it had died, so that Atlantis remained a family tradition, the alleged facts passing from Solon to Plato's kinsman, Dropidas, and thence through the elder Critias, Callaeschrus, and Critias the Younger, to Plato.

Presumably, Critias bequeathed these oral or written notes to his nephew, Plato, who seems to have "edited" these supposed memories and written them down in the dialogues of *Timaeu*s and *Critias*. Classical commentators after Plato's death were in little better position than ourselves to know the truth. Unable to assess the factual content of the Atlantis material, they confined themselves to the philosophical aspects of the material.

According to Proclus (also called Diadochus), an early follower of Plato and a member of the Academy, Crantor, accepted the story of Atlantis as genuinely factual, as did Syrianus, another philosopher of that period. However, Aristotle looked upon Plato's Atlantean writings as mere myth.

It was two centuries before further important commentary was made. Posidonius, Strabo, and Pliny, in the first century B.C., were careful to follow tradition and not to pronounce for or against the possible existence of Atlantis. There was much undoubted geophysical evidence of violent change, so that an island or continent might well have disappeared, and they had no basis for argument against the former existence of Atlantis. Typical of early commentators was Plutarch who regretted that "of all the beautiful works of Plato, the tale of the lost Atlantis has remained unfinished." The early church father Tertullian saw no reason why Atlantis should not have existed in fact and not merely in Plato's imagination.

In the third century A.D., Longinus supported Aristotle's view of Atlantis, but most commentators of that period chose to preserve a measure of doubt. Arnobius the Elder and the historian Ammianus Marcelinus, and the Neoplatonic philosopher Iamblichus were willing to accept the existence of Atlantis on Plato's authority. Two centuries later, their view was upheld by the Byzantine geographer Kosmas Indikopleustes. With the onset of the Dark Ages in the sixth century, there was little addition made to Plato's writing on Atlantis. This lack of interest is to be expected since all knowledge about Atlantis was derived from Plato's two dialogues, which in turn were based on private notes gathered in a distant land. Historical references to the loss of Atlantis were said to have been inscribed on a series of columns in Egypt which were supposed to have still existed a generation after Plato, when the philosopher Crantor saw them and found, according to Proclus, that their texts tallied with Plato's story. Some time afterward, probably when people wished to investigate them for material to augment the *Critias* fragment (the end of the book had in the meantime evidently been lost), the monuments could no longer be traced, and all the Egyptian Atlantis traditions had been forgotten in the general and progressive decay of civilization of the Nile land.

One exception is the sophist Theopompus of Chios, who lived in the fourth century B.C., who told in his book *Philippika* of Meropis, of a marvelous island in the Western Sea, larger than Asia, Libya, and Europe (and hence exceeding Plato's Atlantis in size) whose inhabitants, the Meropes, were builders of large cities and resembled the Atlanteans. However, this work was regarded by ancient commentators as largely a work of fancy, and perhaps was an effort to create a second Atlantis.

Toward the beginning of our era, Diodorus Siculus told in his *Bibliotheke Historike* of an island of not inconsiderable size, which was situated in the Atlantic Ocean off North Africa, several days' sail from the coast. He said it was described as fertile, mountainous, with large, rolling plains, watered by navigable rivers, or perhaps canals.

As Hans Schindler Bellamy points out in his *The Atlantis Myth*, "Altogether about a hundred Atlantis references are found in the post-Platonic classical literature, but they add no new aspects or facets to the great philosopher's myth. Before Plato: silence; after, echoes." Jowett regarded Atlantis as "an island in the clouds which might be seen anywhere by the eye of faith."

Jowett's view, however, like his translations, is colored by his nineteenth-century morality and emphasis on Plato's "scientific" reasoning. Jowett writes: "The jests of the comic poets which have come down to us are indeed harmless enough, and concern the philosopher more than the man; but there are other reproaches, for the silencing of which, Seneca's apology—that the life of a philosopher can never entirely correspond with his doctrine—is scarcely sufficient. On the one hand, he is accused of connections, which, if proved, would forever throw a shadow on his memory; on the other hand of unfriendly, and even of hostile behavior toward several of his fellow disciples. He has also been charged with censoriousness and self-love, not to mention the seditious behavior after the death of Socrates which scandal has laid to his account. His relation with the Syracusan court was early made the handle for diverse accusations, such as the love of pleasure, avarice, flattery of tyrants; and his political character has especially suffered at the hands of those who were themselves unable to grasp his ideas. Lastly, if we were to believe his accusers, he not only, as an author, allowed himself numerous false assertions respecting his predecessors, but also such indiscriminate quotation from their works that a considerable portion of his own writings can be nothing more than a robbery from them."

So eager is Jowett to defend Plato from his accusers that he makes Plato sound like a Victorian gentleman. But Plato was an ancient Greek and must be judged, morally and otherwise, by the standards of his historical time and place. Only by so doing may his writings, and especially those regarding the Atlantean myth, be brought into focus. Let us begin by briefly summing up the main features of the Atlantis material.

In the first place, the gods divided the earth among themselves, proportioning it according to their respective rank. Each established temples to himself, ordained a priestcraft and a system of sacrifice. To Poseidon was given Atlantis. In the middle of the island was a mountain, perhaps a volcano, wherein dwelt three human beings: Evenor, his wife Leucippe, and their beautiful daughter, Cleito. After the death of her parents, Cleito was wooed by Poseidon and begat him five pairs of boys. Atlas, the eldest, ruled over the other nine. Before their birth, Poseidon had divided Atlantis into concentric zones of land and water. Two zones of land and three of water surrounded the central island, which was irrigated by a spring of warm and one of cold water.

Wise government and industry advanced Atlantis beyond surrounding cultures. With apparently unlimited natural resources, the Atlanteans domesticated wild animals, mined precious metals, and distilled perfume. They also erected palaces, temples, and canals and docks. The network of canals united various parts of the kingdom.

Plato then describes the white, black, and red stones which they quarried to build their public constructions. They circumscribed each of the land zones with a wall, the outer wall covered with brass, the middle one with tin, and the inner wall, which encompassed the temple to Poseidon, with ori chalch. The citadel on the central island was surrounded by a wall of gold. Here Poseidon's 10 descendants were born and here they brought offerings. Poseidon's own temple was covered with silver and its pinnacles with gold. The interior was of ivory, gold, silver, and orichalch, even the pillars and floor. A huge statue of Poseidon, standing in a chariot drawn by six winged horses, about him a hundred Nereids riding dolphins, stood in the center of the temple. Outside, were golden statues of the first 10 kings and their wives.

In the groves and gardens were hot and cold springs. There were places for public exercise, public baths, and a great race course. There were fortifications throughout the islands, into whose harbors came ships from every nation in the then known world. So great was the population that the sound of the human voice was forever to be heard.

That portion of Atlantis which faced the sea was lofty and precipitous, but the central city was on a plain surrounded by mountains. Due to the irrigation canals, the plain yielded two crops each year. The plain was divided into 10 sections, each of which was required to yield its quota of men and material during time of war.

The military requirements of each of the 10 communities differed. Each king was sovereign in his own right, but their mutual relationships were governed by a central code engraved on a column of orichalch by the first 10 kings. Each five or six years, pilgrimages were made to the main temple so that appropriate sacrifices could be made, and each king renewed his oath of loyalty upon the sacred inscription. At this time, the kings donned azure robes and sat in judgment. At daybreak, they wrote their sentences upon a golden tablet and left them with their robes as memorials. The chief law of Atlantis was that the kings should not war against each other and that they should mutually defend any one of them who was attacked. In times of crisis, final decisions rested with the direct descendants of Atlas. No king had the power of life and death over his kinsmen without the agreement of a majority of the 10.

Can such a civilization as Atlantis have ever existed? "Not," as Robert Ferro and Michael Grumley put the question in *Atlantis: The Autobiography of a Search*, "did it, or when or where; just could it have existed and what does that mean?"

Plato's narrative is consistent up to the point of the collapse of the empire in a single day, according to Egyptian priests, in 9600 B.C. Atlantis fell through "overweening pride" on the part of its citizens, who were then engaged in attacking both Athens and Egypt. But Athens did not exist in 9600 B.C. Writing and metalworking had not yet come into existence. Farming communities date from about 7000 B.C. and horses were not known in Europe until the Bronze Age. Architecture of the kind Plato describes, including pyramids, did not exist before 4000 B.C.

On the other hand, Aristotle's theory that Atlantis was intended as an allegory to illustrate Plato's political theories does not stand up. The narrative, unlike the *Republic*, espouses no particular theory and reads more like historical fact, however confusing, than a myth. More plausible is the speculation of Edward Bacon, in *Man, Myth and Magic*, who said, "the Atlantis described by Plato was very like what archeology has uncovered of the High Bronze Age civilizations of the Aegean and the Near East—such as the Minoans, the Mycenaeans, the Hittites, the Egyptians, and the Babylonians—between about 2500 and 1200 B.C. Was there, then, something wrong with Plato's date? Had the Egyptian priests or Solon confused 900 with 9,000 years? If so, the date of the disaster would be 1500 B.C. instead of 9600 B.C."

This assumption makes the existence of Atlantis and its subsequent destruction much more credible. A volcanic cataclysm is known to have occurred during the empire of Minoan Crete in about the sixteenth century B.C. The Minoan civilization collapsed from a series of natural disasters, fires, floods, and earthquakes. It was about that time, that Santorini (Thera) suffered a volcanic explosion about five times as great as that of Krakatoa in 1883, which was heard in San Francisco and sent tidal waves across the entire Pacific. Bacon concludes: "These two accounts of unparalleled disaster are so similar in nature, location and date that they must be different accounts of the same disaster. And when an archeological expedition, led by Professor Marinatos of Athens, uncovered in 1967 Minoan remains deep under the pumice of Santorini, the final link was added and the identification of Santorini with the Ancient Metropolis of Atlantis, and of Minoan Crete with the Royal City and empire of the Atlanteans, became virtually inevitable."

However, the merely historical evidence of Atlantis leaves unexplained a major question: Why did Plato bother to write about it? Plato was not a historian, and there is nothing in his other writings to indicate that he would have taken any interest in a purely historical Atlantis. We must then seek an additional and more occult explanation of the Atlantis myth.

The doyen of modern American occultists, Manly P. Hall, in *The Secret Teachings of All Ages*, comments that, "From a careful consideration of Plato's description of Atlantis it is evident that the story should not be regarded as wholly historical but rather as both allegorical and historical." He continues, "Origen, Porphyry, Proclus, Iamblichus, and Syrianus realized that the story concealed a profound philosophical mystery, but they disagreed as to the actual interpretation. Plato's Atlantis symbolizes the threefold nature of both the universe and the human body. The 10 kings of Atlantis are the *Tetractys* [referring to the arithmetical fact that 1, 2, 3, and 4 equal 10], which are born as five pairs of opposites. (Consult Theon of Smyrna for the Pythagorean doctrine of opposites.) The numbers of 1 to 10 rule every creature, and the numbers, in turn, are under the control of the Monad, or 1—the elder among them.

"With the trident scepter of Poseidon these kings held sway over the inhabitants of the seven small and three great islands comprising Atlantis. Philosophically, the ten islands symbolize the triune powers of the Superior Deity and the seven regents who bow before his eternal throne. If Atlantis be considered as the archetypal sphere, then its immersion signifies the descent of rational, organized consciousness into the illusionary, impermanent realm of irrational mortal ignorance. Both the sinking of Atlantis and the biblical story of the "fall of man" signify spiritual involution—a prerequisite to conscious evolution.

"Either the initiated Plato used the Atlantis allegory to achieve two widely different ends or else the accounts preserved by the Egyptian priests were tampered with to perpetuate the secret doctrine. This does not mean to imply that Atlantis is purely mythological, but it overcomes the most serious obstacle to the acceptance of the Atlantis story, namely the fantastic accounts of its origin, size, appearance, and date of destruction—9600 B.C. In the midst of the central island of Atlantis was a lofty mountain which cast a shadow five thousand stadia in length and whose summit touched the sphere of aether. This is the axle mountain of the world, sacred among many races and symbolic of the human head, which rises out of the four elements of the body. This sacred mountain, upon whose summit stood the temple of the gods, gave rise to the stories of Olympus, Meru and Asgard. The City of the Golden Gates—the capital of Atlantis—is the one now preserved among numerous religions as the 'City of the Gods' or the 'Holy City.' Here is the archetype of the 'New Jerusalem,' with its streets paved with gold and its twelve gates shining with precious stones."

CHAPTER 3

Impact on Egypt

People who fear or survive a cataclysm move. The thing that makes them move is the need to survive. In the act of attempting to survive, they become aggressive and fiercely competitive. They pose a threat to others whose way of life has not been disrupted. Trouble follows until the survivors have been absorbed.

The greater a cataclysm, the more people will be in motion. If the cataclysm was great enough, those displaced will form hordes of significant power. Edmund Burke, the British statesman, said that public calamity was a great leveler. People in distress tend to forget their differences and cling together, their animal instincts prevailing over ideologies. They form into an army that has but one objective, to gain a secure livelihood—even if that means upsetting the security of the more fortunate.

If the blowup of Thera and its impact on Crete (or Atlantis) was severe enough, it would have set such an army in motion. If earthquakes and floods accompanied the eruption, the area involved in the cataclysm would have been greater and the numbers of people affected proportionately larger. Such a migration would have left its mark on the recorded history of Mediterranean peoples who escaped the disaster. Its impact would define a period of migration and strife involving extensive sections of the Mediterranean littoral. Very likely the start of the period would be marked by records of extraordinary natural occurrences—spin-off and secondary effects of the primary cataclysm.

Is it possible to identify such a period? It seems so. One such period can be specifically identified, although there may have been several Thera eruptions. The period seems to have begun at the time of transition from the 19th to the 20th dynasties in Egypt, although authorities differ on the exact

19

calendar years involved. Such an era began in the last third of the fourteenth century B.C., the time of the death of Pharaoh Ramses II, the latter part of whose reign was an extended period of peace.

At this time, the major powers in the Eastern Mediterranean sector were Egypt, the Hittite Empire in Lebanon and Asia Minor, and the Chaldeans, then under the Kassites. Egypt and Chaldea had never had any serious trouble and the Hittites were allied to Egypt by a treaty Ramses II had signed. Things were quiet on the region's international scene.

But there was unrest inside Egypt. The priests of Amon disliked the way that Ramses seemed to prefer the god Set, and foreign laborers—including some known as the Habiru—complained that they were oppressed in their task of building the delta cities of Pithom and Ramses. However, the Pharaoh, a man given to direct action, had things under control.

Ramses was succeeded by his thirteenth son, Merneptah. Never did a new pharaoh have bigger sandals to fill. His father had been a man of great personal courage and public charisma. Merneptah tried to bolster his own image by copying the grandiose style of Ramses' inscriptions and imitated his extensive building programs. He was, in spite of this, regarded as somewhat of a pushover, particularly by his Libyan neighbors.

It may have been Merneptah's lack of a strong image that prompted the Pithom and Ramses labor battalions to flee. They may have been hastened by unusual storms, quakes, precipitations, and other phenomena that seem to have broken out at once. The Habiru fled Egypt along with a mixed multitude (*Exodus* 12:38.).

The nature of the phenomena has been described in the Bible and in Hebrew tradition. The major ones involved, by any interpretation at all, strong winds, darkness, a hail of cinders, earthquakes, and tidal waves—just what we could expect in Egypt if the Thera eruption reached the magnitude attributed to it.

It would seem, though, that these manifestations were only those of a preliminary eruption and seismic disturbance. In an estimated seven weeks, the fleeing Hebrews were before the mountain designated in the Bible as Mount Sinai. Though there is some doubt as to whether it was located in the mountains along the eastern shore of the Red Sea or in Edom

(Mount Seir), this matter is not important to us here. What concerns us is the nature of what the Israelites observed.

According to *Exodus*, the mountain was "altogether on a smoke" that ascended "like the smoke of a furnace." Later accounts describe the mountain as quaking so violently that it seemed to be shaken above the spectators. There was lightning, thunder, hailstones, and coals of fire. There was a great darkness. And there was a sound like that of a mighty trumpet.

Stripped of biblical vernacular, the events attendant upon the Exodus and the appearance before the Mount of the lawgiving describe what we would expect as consequences of an earthquake and volcanic upheaval in the Eastern Mediterranean basin, with reverberations in Egypt, on the Sinai Peninsula and inland, perhaps, in Edom.

While there are many evidences that could be marshaled to support this interpretation of the exodus phenomena—the *naos* of el-Arish, the Arabian accounts of Masudi, and so on—the point here is to relate the observed phenomena with signs of movement on the part of displaced people.

Those who place the exodus in the earliest part of Merneptah's reign may well be justified. In his fourth year, Egypt was hit by the Libyans who had formed a confederation with a mysterious "People of the Sea." Libya was always a problem to Egypt: always beaten, it refused to take its defeats seriously, and kept trying again and again. This time, with its new allies, it tried once more, only to suffer yet another defeat at the hands of Merneptah's chariot-borne archers. When the battle on the West Delta was over, the Pharaoh ordered all his prisoners to be branded with his name and, while this was going on, offered them a chance to work off his royal displeasure. How would they like to be settled in military camps and protect Egypt from marauding nomads in South Palestine? They would, and they went about it aggressively. Merneptah went to his tomb a somewhat do-nothing pharaoh compared with his father. Even his inscriptions failed him, one recording jubilantly: "Israel is dead and has no seed." He had had no further trouble with the Sea People and their reappearance was not to be till three decades had passed; unless, in the upheavals that shook Egypt in that time, their occasional raids passed unnoticed.

Pharaoh Seti II took over and reigned for six years, being

the last of the 19th dynasty. Egyptian scribes, always vague where bad news was concerned (they never even recorded judicial death sentences except in some kind of euphemism like "He was judged by Pharaoh and the judges agreed with Pharaoh . . ."), do not record the circumstances in which a man named Siptah became the first Pharaoh of the 20th dynasty. He only lasted six years. Then his wife, Tawosret, took over. She even took over Siptah's inscriptions, too, changing many of them to read as though she had ruled as king (the Egyptians had no word for queen) since his first regnal year. Her actual reign was two years.

There was a brief interregnum by a Syrian usurper, and then Setnakht became pharaoh. He took over Tawosret's tomb as his own, though he sired Ramses III before he occupied it.

Ramses III was the last great pharaoh of Egypt. He took over a country that had been divided by riot and civil war and tried to restore it to its former splendor. He had hardly started, when he received the traditional bad news from the Libyan frontier. This time the Libyans said Ramses had interfered in the succession of one of their chieftains, and they were going to attack. They attacked with the usual results. The prisoners were branded with Ramses' name and settled in military camps. Occasionally Ramses would use them to fight against raids by their own kin.

Two years later there was more bad news, this time from the eastern frontier. The People of the Sea had returned with a vastly augmented force and were camped at Amor in Syria. Thanks to Ramses' inscriptions in his mortuary temple at Madinat Habu, we know where the Sea People had been and what they had been doing. They had overrun the powerful Hittite Empire and effectively wiped it from the face of the earth. Now they were marshaling at Amor and their land army had a naval arm. Trailed by their families and cattle, the People of the Sea began to march on Egypt. Archers on their ships covered the land advance.

In two thousand years of history since its kingdoms were united, Egypt had never fought a sea battle. Its people were simply not seafarers, and some writers have alleged that the Egyptians had a superstitious dread of the sea. Piloting on the Nile was a different matter. The Nile was the main artery of Egypt and it was policed by a kind of highway patrol known as the White Flame. *White* was the color of purity, nobility, and righteousness; *flame* connoted vengeance, punishment, and retribution.

When the Egyptian army sallied forth to meet the Sea People, the White Flame went with them along the Pelusiac branch of the Nile. The details of the battle that followed are lost, though murals at Madinat Habu tell a good deal about it. The ships of the White Flame, their drafts shallow for navigation in a silted Nile, were ideally suited for close-in coverage of the army from offshore. In combat with other ships, they had a peculiar military advantage, a tall mast surmounted by a kind of crow's nest which sheltered archers. Archers so placed had the advantage of firing downwards at their targets. Some historians assert that units of the White Flame led ships of the Sea People into treacherous branches of the Nile, waited until they ran aground and then came about with a fatal rain of arrows.

On shore the Egyptian army, always well disciplined and skilled with the short sword, flail, javelin, and bow attacked the vanguard of the Sea People. In looking at the Madinat Habu inscriptions we get the impression that men of the same armament did not always fight together in units. It appears more likely that cadres were made up of, say, a swordsman, an archer, and a javelin specialist. Then there were the chariots manned by a driver and an archer and pulled by warhorses trained to penetrate to the thick of the fray—a maneuver that seems to have been devised by Ramses II, who almost lost his life demonstrating it at the Battle of Kadesh.

Except for the few who fled, those of the Sea People not killed were captured. The inscriptions tell us something of their identities. There were the Akaiwasha who have been associated with the Archaean Greeks. The Pelescti became the Philistines of the Bible. There were also the Tjekker and the Turusa that no one is quite sure about yet. The Peleseti are the most easily identified on the Madinat inscriptions, if only because of their headgear which has some resemblance to the American Indians' war bonnet. Along with the Tjekkers, they were settled in military camps on the Palestine coast between Gaza and Mount Carmel. Eventually they became independent of Egypt.

Ramses III reigned for another 25 years. Though Egypt

held its own, he was never able to restore the ancient glories. It had become riddled with corruption from within. By Ramses' time we begin to find the names of foreigners in high positions at court. Some, like that of Iun Turusa, suggest that at least a few of the Sea People had found favor in Egyptian government circles. Egypt's might had begun to fade.

The Hittites were destroyed. In Chaldea, the Kassites had all but lost their power and would disappear from history in a couple of decades. It was in this era that fabled Troy fell to the Achaeans. New settlers moved into the Grecian mainland and called their territory Doris. They are known to us as the Dorian Greeks; they took over the Peloponnesus and, in Argolis, destroyed Mycenae.

At this time the Etruscans entered Italy. Herodotus said they came from Lydia, in flight from famine. Lydia and Troas (the site of Troy) made up Anatolia, the heartland of the vanished Hittites whom we know were overrun by the Sea People. A century after the era under discussion here, the district would become the Kingdom of Phrygia, though it had been settled as early as the thirteenth century B.C. by "people of uncertain origin"—according to *Webster's Geographical Dictionary*.

A remarkable thing about the Etruscans is that we have never learned to translate their language, though we can read it: they used a form of the Greek alphabet. But more remarkable is the fact that favorite toys or charms or doodads among the Etruscans bore the alphabet as a decorative device. Now, your cigarette lighter or your fountain pen is not decorated with the ABC's: that would be meaningless because there would be no novelty to it. One may wonder, then, if perhaps the Greek alphabet was so unfamiliar to the Etruscans that they needed to carry about *aides-memoires* to help them get used to it. And, if so, what was their original alphabet? Could it have been one of the undeciphered scripts from Knossos? Or from some other land now sunk below the Sea of Candia?

In this chapter we have assumed that certain conditions would prevail if a major cataclysm devastated a portion of the Eastern Mediterranean. We sought then for a historical period when those conditions seemed to exist and we found them at the end of the thirteenth and the beginning of the twelfth centuries B.C.

Having, as we do, evidence of one or several major eruptions of Thera, it seems reasonable to relate it to the pattern of conditions we have renewed. The eruptions of Thera may have caused the migrations and their far-reaching economic and social impact. Where written records are absent, the forceful movement of peoples offers its own dramatic evidence.

CHAPTER 4

At the Center of the Center

Spyridon Marinatos was a single-minded, impatient man. The archaeological diggings and scrapings at Thera were going too slowly for him. And then a wall of the emerging site crumbled, and it crushed and killed him. This was in 1973. But his work was continued by others; in 1976 the final studies by Professor Marinatos were published in Athens under the simple title, *Excavations at Thera VII*, the seventh of a series, covering the 1973 season. "At the moment of the devastating catastrophe" that was caused by the gigantic eruption of the island, Marinatos wrote, "practically every building has deviated from the vertical." This made digging, protecting finds, and even the safety of the archaeologists risky. The district of Akrotiri, target of Marinatos' effort since he first saw it as the key to the island's past in 1939, has yielded numerous finds; but risks and costs remained high.

Several newly discovered, beautifully colored frescoes were located during Marinatos' last season on Thera. One was of a group of young women gathering crocuses, filling baskets, and emptying them. Perhaps these were part of an offering to a divinity. Marinatos wrote that "the existence of a sanctuary or altar is to be imagined nearby, because another three women painted in natural size carry huge bunches of flowers against their bosom." The representation, he added, "is astonishing because each of the seven figures forms an individual composition of incredible daring and originality." Elsewhere, frescoes show ducks flying amidst reeds, "while smaller birds have been apparently caught in nets." The two most delightful figures in the frescoes are "linked and enlivened by the theme of their conversation. The young girls met while wandering in the meadow and are now exchanging some typically feminine remarks . . ."

Even a fact-devoted archaeologist may be permitted an occasional flight of fancy: reconstructing a conversation among girls on a sunny day long before our own records of history. The ruins of the Minoan type (until then largely restricted to Crete) are in the Akrotiri area. Next to Marinatos', the ideas of Professor A. G. Galanapoulos have influenced scientific and public thought concerning links of Thera to the Atlantis legend. An American oceanographic engineer, one of the designers of the famous submarine *Alvin* that found a missing H-bomb off the coast of Spain, has rounded these out still further; he is Dr. James W. Mavor, Jr., of the Woods Hole Oceanographic Institution on Cape Cod. In his book *Voyage to Atlantis* (1969), Mavor summarized the Galanapoulos position: Thera did not just blow up and cause tidal waves that destroyed an Atlantis that was, in actual fact, Crete; rather, Thera *was* Atlantis! Its very center, now a crater filled with water, was the city-state that indirectly inspired Plato, Mavor believes.

In his book, Mavor wrote that the "eruption and collapse of Thera was truly an earthshaking event capable of destroying an Atlantis reduced to a manageable size from the exaggerated dimensions reported by Plato." Mavor suggested that "the Atlantis myth is the central one of a great body of related myths pertaining to the great Thera destruction, the Minoans and their sea empire, the Mycenaean Greeks and their conflicts with the Minoans and the origins of the Aegean people." In his view, "the Atlantis story can lead us to an understanding of the migrations and other cultural dispersions of Near Eastern and European peoples as far from the Aegean, conceivably, as the British Isles."

Writing in the Swiss archaeological journal, *Antike Welt* (*World of Antiquity*), Mavor restated in an article, "Journey to Atlantis" (Vol. 1, No. 4, 1970), Galanopoulos' concept of a central metropolis within the Thera complex, a small circular island with an easily accessible port. With his background in submarine research, Mavor was particularly interested in reaching underwater ruins that had been inaccessible for 3,-500 years. This submarine expedition had to wait, particularly as Marinatos showed a certain ambivalence toward projects not directly under his control.

Although Thera's fate has been known for a long time, and although the Atlantis legend might well have led to an earlier exploration of the island's geological background, inquiries are of very recent date. This is understandable when one recalls that only about a century ago, in 1867, a French engineer using volcanic ash in building the Suez Canal, published a work called *Santorini et ses éruptions.* Historians and archaeologists shared ignorance of Minoan civilization (named after the mythical King Minos), as the Cretan diggings had not yet taken place, and the Palace of Knossos, in all its beauty, was still unknown.

The experts differ on the actual meaning of the beautifully executed, elegantly stylish frescoes found on the Santorini excavation site of Akrotiri. They are strikingly similar to those unearthed earlier at the Palace of Knossos in Crete. How can you and I, mere laymen, come to grips with the realities behind their academic arguments? Our best bet, it seems to me, is to listen to an appraisal by a man who is himself a scholar, but who stands outside the dispute over the role Santorini played in the story of Atlantis.

In this case, we can turn to Dr. D. L. Page, a British scholar who is Regius Professor of Greek and Master of Jesus College at Cambridge, England. Professor Page is a skilled referee, able to appraise the different arguments as an outsider; he modestly calls himself "an amateur in the field" of archaeology, but he is a Hellenic scholar of worldwide prestige. In 1969, he attended the so-called "Thera Congress" in Greece, an international scientific conference that dealt with "all aspects of the Santorini volcano."

In his book, *The Santorini Volcano and the Destruction of Minoan Crete,* published in 1970 by the Society for the Promotion of Hellenic Studies, London, Page examined the evidence and conclusions, step by step. I can agree, from personal observation, with his statement that on the island of Santorini "you see plain evidence of one of the biggest volcanic eruptions on earth since the last ice age," whereas in Crete "you find that almost every place in its eastern half which was inhabited in a certain period was destroyed in that period." Was there, he asked, a cause and effect? Was "Minoan Crete destroyed by the action of the volcano at Santorini"? What are the "basic facts on which a conclusion must be based"?

Going over the evidence on Crete, Professor Page examined the nature and periods of finds on various archaeological sites. He differentiated between three different art styles prominent on Crete during the second millennium B.C., the so-called Floral Style (with decorative flowers prominent), the Marine Style (which showed themes of the sea), and, finally, the Palace Style, of which Knossos is the best known and most imposing example. He noted that authorities differ in placing the destruction of various edifices on the large island. He concluded that "the general catastrophe occurred about the middle of the fifteenth century, and that Knossos, although its palace was damaged, survived the catastrophe at that time and was quite soon restored to prosperity."

Crete, it would seem from this and other data, suffered a series of devastating blows—it wasn't just one earthquake, or possibly an outside invasion (this seems very doubtful), but a series of quakes and shocks, tremors, and sea quakes—all of which did severe damage, capped by the volcanic outbreak of Santorini. Page felt that an earthquake alone, without volcanic activity, "is not a probable answer to our question," because an earthquake "might account for the destruction, but not for the abandonment" of major parts of Crete.

Now, going on from the assumption that "the greater part of eastern Crete was destroyed and abandoned within a short space of time," around the mid-fifteenth century B.C., Page examined Santorini as "actually in the past, as potentially in the future, one of the most violent volcanoes in the history of the earth." What happened to Santorini was not, as we know by now, a sudden overnight eruption that virtually destroyed the island and had enormous repercussions on Crete and elsewhere—rather, the destruction took place in stages that are now clearly visible. The first major eruption of the volcano resulted in the ejection of an enormous mass of pumice; we know this substance in our daily use as "pumice stone," an abrasive material contained in many scouring compounds. Actually, pumice is volcanic glass filled with air bubbles.

Even as you approach Santorini harbor, you can distinguish the multicolored rock that reflects the layers placed by volcanic action. Santorini shows between 12 and 15 feet of pumice, topped by a colored ribbon—a sort of buffer zone—that is three to four feet in height. And finally, there is a top layer of 60 to 75 feet of volcanic ash. Professor Page describes the volcanic process that produced this "layer cake" as follows:

"The material ejected in a volcanic eruption consists of

'magma'—molten rock charged with gases. Magma issues from the volcano mainly in two ways: by flowing as a stream of lava; or by violent ejection in the form of bombs, pumice, and ash. Volcanic bombs are lumps of magma ejected and solidified as lava in passage through air. The great bulk of the material violently ejected upward consists of pumice and ash. Pumice is the froth on top of the magma; when the gas-content of the magma is very high, the surface turns to froth as the magma rises up the cone into zones of decreasing pressure, and the frothy surface is blown upwards in the form of pumice. Volcanic ash is pumice reduced to minute particles, consisting mainly of glass."

We cannot let these details bore us or ignore them, because they are essential to an understanding of the relation between the Santorini outbreak and the fate of Crete. What is involved here, Page tells us, is evidence to show that "the volcanic activity was of this and not of some other type," because only this type of eruption "may cause destruction at a great distance from its centre." He calls Santorini "a classic example of the type; visible here are the huge deposits of pumice and ash and the disintegrated volcano."

Each year we hear of earthquakes and floods that kill and endanger large numbers of people. In 1976 alone, quakes hit mainland China, the Philippines, Turkey, and a French island in the Caribbean. The constant adjustment of pressure within the earth's crust makes for interrelated cataclysms, of which sea floods are a major factor. These are known in the literature of the field as *tsunamis*; a *tsunami*—a Japanese term—is precisely the kind of overwhelming and devastating sea disturbance that precedes, accompanies, or follows an earthquake or volcanic action. If Santorini was the origin of Crete's partial destruction, a *tsunami* probably was the major cause of damages to the island's shore and may even be responsible for the actual disappearance of parts of Crete beneath the sea.

Professor Page states: "The magnitude of the final paroxysm of Santorini—that which left the great ash-layer and broke the mountain down—was such that a land so close as Crete will be severely damaged if it lay in the path of the ash cloud and the sea-floods." When I first visited Santorini, viewing the island from the sea within the caldera, I was unprepared for the actual, vast size of the oval shape that had been the volcano's crater. Page noted that "the volume of rock displaced at Santorini was much greater than in other volcanic eruptions from that day to this." In other words, the sheer mass material thrown out from the innards of the earth was so enormous as to be just about unimaginable, and the damage it must have caused is therefore equally incalculable.

The layers of various building sites, household items, and decorative pieces, together with the levels of pumice and ash on Santorini and Crete make it difficult to prove that the volcanic outbreak coincided with the disintegration of Minoan civilization. Volcanologists have found that the time which usually elapses between earth tremors and the actual major outbreak of a volcano must be measured in days, weeks, and possibly months—but the lapse of a decade or two, as some of the evidence indicates, is unlikely.

That earthquakes hit Crete repeatedly is not in doubt. Three major palaces, at Knossos, Phaestros and Mallia, as well as many other structures, collapsed about 1700 B.C. But, Page points out, while subsequent major quakes shook the island of Crete, at least a decade elapsed between the destruction of the Santorini settlements and those of Crete: "The archaeological evidence requires two volcanic eruptions separated by an interval of this order of magnitude—one eruption depositing the great pumice-layer and burying the Santorini habitations, another of much greater violence at a later date depositing the huge layer of ash on Santorini and causing the desolation of Crete."

The pattern of Santorini devastations has, in fact, been one whereby earthquakes were followed by volcanic eruptions, although not in all cases. Serious volcanic activity took place in 236 B.C., separating what is now the island of Therasia from northwestern Santorini. There was a four day eruption in 197 B.C.; this one produced the Palea Kaimeni isle that later rose to its present height of 330 feet in the center of the Santorini caldera. Sometime during the first century A.D., a small island briefly appeared in the caldera. In the year 726, a major volcanic eruption sent pumice clouds as far as Asia Minor (now Turkey) and Macedonia (northern Greece).

In relatively recent times, 1570, Santorini's south coast collapsed and the ancient port of Eleusis sank beneath the sea; it may have been founded by the Phoenicians. Three years later, an eruption within the caldera created a small oval-shaped island, about 220 feet high, called Mikra Kaimeni ("Small Burned Island"). A fairly contemporary equivalent to the prehistoric cataclysm took place in 1650, when a series of quakes preceded a submarine eruption off the northeast coast of the island. A small island was formed by lava, and several *tsunamis* damaged virtually all other Aegean islands. Poisonous gas blinded and killed people, livestock, and wild animals on Santorini itself. An earthquake preceded the eruption by two weeks.

We are not, by any means, dealing with a volcanic island that is quiescent. Between 1707 and 1711, an explosion created Nea Kaimeni within the caldera. And a series of volcanic eruptions during the last century, from 1866 to 1870, created several small islands, of which two were joined to Nea Kaimeni. The eruption hurled pumice as far as Crete.

Mikra Kaimeni disappeared as a separate entity as late as the nineteen-twenties. Beginning in August 1925, 100 million cubic feet of lava filled much of the channel between Mikra Kaimeni and Nea Kaimeni. The eruption lasted until May 1926. Two years later, a new explosion completed the molding together of the two small islands. The volcano on Nea Kaimeni was active from 1939 to 1941, with lava adding to its surface. Another eruption continued this movement in 1950.

In 1956, Santorini was the major victim of a quake that affected all of the Aegean area; on the island itself, 48 people were killed, hundreds injured, some 1,000 houses destroyed. Minor tremors continue to this day, and gases escape from volcanic cracks within the caldera region.

As Page notes, there is "nothing unprecedented in the hypothesis of a devastating earthquake in Crete accompanied by conflagrations and followed quite soon by an exceptionally violent eruption of the Santorini volcano." The nineteenth-century outbreaks on Santorini, noted above, were paralleled by quake action on Crete, notably on October 12, 1865; only 18 of 3,620 houses were left standing in the town of Heraklion. Professor Page comments: "The only difference was magnitude; the modern scale was large, the ancient was colossal."

If the disasters that hit Minoan civilization on prehistoric Crete came in intermittent waves, rather than in one major cataclysm, the same appears to have been the case on Santorini. The island's major excavation site, which I visited in 1976, is in the village of Akrotiri; begun by Professor Spyridon Marinatos, it is being continued under the direction of his former deputy, Dr. Christos Doumas. The excavations revealed, quite clearly, that this Minoan-type settlement experienced a major disaster, was severely damaged, but later reoccupied by what the archaeologists call "squatters." In other words, the impressive temples, workshops, storehouses, and living quarters of Akrotiri collapsed during what was surely an earthquake—whether or not accompanied by a volcanic explosion—and the inhabitants, or other people, went back to the damaged structures and lived in them without proper rebuilding, until another disaster struck. These "squatters" tunneled their way into or below collapsed structures and set up relatively primitive housekeeping in buildings that had been buried in pumice and ash.

Professor Marinatos, in his first report on these findings, *Excavations at Thera, I: First Preliminary Report; 1967 Season* (Athens, 1968) summarized the hypothesis that "attributed the great destruction of Minoan Crete around 1500 B.C. to a vast eruption of the Thera-volcano." This concept, Marinatos stated, found in the Akrotiri excavations support for its overall recreation of these events of 3,500 years ago:

"Crete would have been destroyed by a series of tidal waves and by repeated earthquakes. The majority of the inhabitants would have abandoned the island. The palaces were destroyed and went out of use forever with the exception of the Palace of Knossos, which, however was inhabited by a new Achaean dynasty. The expatriate Minoans fled to every part of the Mediterranean, especially to Mainland Greece and particularly to the Western Peloponnese. They transplanted their art and religion and culture to Mycenaean Greece. The last surviving palatial scribes of Crete offered their services to the courts of the more powerful Mycenean rulers."

Marinatos then refers to what remains one of the great mysteries in the history of language, the so-called Linear B script found in Crete, which has only partly—and with much scholarly controversy—been deciphered. Professor Marinatos wrote that the Cretan scribes "adapted their script to the Greek language," with the first attempt certainly made at Knossos.

Details aside, Marinatos' remark that the Minoans went to

"every part" of the Mediterranean, contains distinct echoes of the Atlantis legend, which assumes that some inhabitants of this doomed island-continent escaped, taking their skills and culture with them to other parts of the world. Looking at the devastation that issued from Santorini around 1550 B.C., and which Professor Page describes as "colossal," compared with all recent devastations since then, there can be no doubt that if Minoan civilization was the center of a cataclysm that gave rise to the Atlantis myth, then Santorini was the very center of this center—from the caldera of this island volcano, in ever-widening circles of destruction, the world as it was then known to the inhabitants of this region was destroyed, its inhabitants scattered to the four winds, much of their cultural accomplishments abandoned, but much also transmitted into the mainstream of skills, ideas, and images that has since become our own Western civilization.

CHAPTER 5

Jacques Cousteau's
Search for Atlantis

The *Calypso*, the shiny, expertly equipped ship under the command of French undersea explorer Jacques Cousteau, lies anchored in the main Greek harbor, Piraeus. It stands out among hundreds of larger and smaller vessels because of its sophisticated deep-sea diving gear, its electronic scanning apparatus—and, above all, because of its master's international renown as a submarine pioneer. For decades, the name of Cousteau has been synonymous with underwater searches ranging from the Indian Ocean to obscure and isolated coastal civilizations in South America.

Cousteau is indisputably this century's most effective link between the undersea world, invisible and unknown to most of us, and a vast audience of viewers, listeners, and readers. Jacques Ives Cousteau was born on June 11, 1910, at St. André-de-Culzac, and identifies himself in biographical directories simply as a "marine explorer." After French naval services in various ranks, he became director of the Oceanographic Museum at Monaco, where he has worked in close contact with Prince Rainier to make the museum, as well as the Institut Océanographique, a unique center of marine research. A key event in Cousteau's life was his development of the aqualung, in 1943, which has been instrumental in making undersea life an open frontier of fascinating new knowledge. In 1957, Jacques Cousteau promoted the Conshelf Saturation Direct Program; his researches have gained increased importance as the world's nations seek to exploit mineral deposits on the ocean floors.

Now, as we see the *Calypso* stopping for repairs and fresh supplies in Piraeus, we can observe with what experience and meticulous care its explorations and their resulting films, television shows, and photographs are prepared. Cousteau, in late

1975 and all through 1976, crisscrossed the Eastern Mediterranean in preparation of a television series "In Search of Atlantis—Lost Civilization."

Asked about the dramatic theme of these films, Jacques Cousteau is cautious. Despite the title, they are designed to advance knowledge of underwater archaeology, rather than perpetuate what Cousteau regards as "the Atlantis myth." His theme, "reality is more gripping than phantasy," underlines that historical and contemporary facts need no embroidery by legend. Much of Cousteau's Atlantis film knits together the dramatic history of the island of Santorini—its volcanic outbursts, rapidly changing geology, impact on the Minoan civilization of Crete, and its current role as the center of the Atlantis controversy.

Yet, Cousteau does not conclude that Atlantis, as such, actually existed. While he described his exploration as an effort to "find the origin of the Atlantean myth," he did not see it as "a search for the lost Atlantis." Rather, he added, "We are interested in all civilizations that once existed but that disappeared, suddenly and without a trace."

The most challenging aspect of *Calypso*'s deep-sea exploration was an exploration of the Santorini caldera, the sunken crater of its volcano. Earlier divers, examining the caldera in 1963, had reported seeing columns, glass-like walls and fish that appeared to have lost all external color, perhaps due to chemical elements in the crater's water. The Greek National Tourist Organization, outlining the Cousteau expedition's aims, stated: "Santorini's history, the civilization that was lost during its terrible volcanic catastrophe, is more significant and moving than a mythical Sunken Continent. And the archaeological treasures which have emerged from the sea in Antikythira [an island located about halfway between Crete and the southern coast of the Peloponnese], Crete, and Delos [west of the widely known island of Mikonos], are more important and impressive than the hypothetical treasures the pirate La Boz is said to have hidden on the Seychelle Islands [in the Indian Ocean]. Atlantis represents the search for a lost idol, a myth of worldwide character."

Thus, while using the theme of Atlantis and of "lost treasures" but treating them as myths, the Cousteau explorations have been able to attract wide public attention, although limiting their scope to more or less scientific aims. Using sophisticated depth-measuring equipment, magnetometers, and radar-like scanners, the *Calypso* roamed the Aegean Sea and examined off-shore areas selected by archaeologists, either because earlier searches had indicated the existence of undersea structures or because the presence of sunken ships was known or suspected.

Heavy seas, muddy waters, and limited visibility hampered Cousteau at various points. Nevertheless, potentially significant findings were reported by the French explorer, notably off the tiny island of Dia, just north of the major Cretan port city of Heraklion. Jacques Cousteau announced that undersea searches in the Dia area had resulted in "a most important find," related to the volcanic history of Santorini and the collapse of Minoan civilization on Crete.

Dia lies due south of Santorini; the waters between the two islands may conceal extensive archaeological treasures. The Greek Ministry of Science and Culture specifically created a Division of Undersea Explorations to encourage and direct submarine archaeology. Cousteau's Dia search brought a number of objects to the surface, strongly similar to those found in Crete and Santorini; these, he said, "point to a civilization that suddenly disappeared." Dia is a picturesque island, with a charming little chapel, populated only by a few shepherds and their flocks. Cousteau observed that Dia gives evidence "it's inhabitants disappeared, either as a result of the tremendous catastrophe at Thera [Santorini], or because of overpopulation; but evidence of their civilization remains in the depths of the sea."

The *Calypso* search around Dia resulted in the location and identification of only 12 vessels, which were taken to the Heraklion Museum. The Cousteau expedition limited its removal of actual objects from undersea structures to samples that might help to pinpoint more extensive future search targets. The French explorer pointed to the presence of sand and mud, which would have to be removed with special mining and suction equipment. Obviously, the Cousteau expedition only laid the groundwork for more extensive, carefully prepared explorations. In close cooperation with his son Philippe, Jacques Cousteau undertook the *Calypso* search in a manner that combined the Greek government's desire to publicize its historic Aegean islands with his own personal touch of showmanship, as well as scientific progress in underwater archaeology; the year-by-year follow-up work may have to be undertaken by less flamboyant marine archaeologists.

The Cousteau search began in November 1975 in the northern zones, including a search off Cape Sounion, the peninsula south of Athens that is topped by the ancient Temple of Apollo. This was followed by explorations in the eastern Aegean and near Crete. A second search, following a servicing of the *Calypso* in Piraeus harbor, concentrated on the discovery of shipwrecks as well as other undersea structures. Some ceramic pieces were collected by the Cousteau team, but no large shipwrecks were found: the French explorer attributed this to "the competence of the seafarers during these early days."

The survey off Antikythira, mentioned above, resulted in finds dating back to the first century A.D. Cousteau paid tribute to Greek divers who had pioneered submarine research in this area as long ago as 1901, at which time a strikingly forceful copper statue of a racing horse, with a young boy as its rider, was discovered; this fascinating example of sculptural skill, conveying motion and grace, is now at the National Archaeological Museum in Athens. At the same time, divers brought up a calculator-type of device which had been used by sailors to chart the stars and possibly to measure time.

Cousteau located a shipwreck in this sea but noted that its exploration "demanded good weather conditions, which did not prevail." He praised the work of the 1901 divers, calling their achievements remarkable and adding that his own search had found no traces of this earlier undertaking, "except for two iron rods they had used to dislodge statues." The gigantic marble statue of a horse, according to Cousteau, "is located at great depth, and although we reached it within one day, weather conditions made detailed searches impossible."

Weather conditions were considerably better when the *Calypso* reached Crete, where it used Heraklion as its base of operations. The island's southern shore was well protected against winds. One recent shipwreck, apparently a Turkish vessel, was located by the team. During the week the Cousteau expedition devoted to the little island of Dia, it discovered five shipwrecks that Cousteau dated to the first and second century A.D.

The Dia search provided evidence of an ancient port, now submerged beneath the sea. Jacques Cousteau spoke of Dia as possibly having been "the key to Crete, thousands of years ago, with a large population." Dia contains considerable evidence of Minoan culture, although a "study of these ruins would require years of work," according to Cousteau. Photographs of the sea bottom revealed ancient structures elsewhere; Minoan ceramic pots were found stuck to rocks, where they "create huge bulks"; receptacles dating back to Roman times were also sighted. The research team discovered "a ship loaded with pillars, from a later period." Minoan ceramic vessels were found in the bay of the island of Ermoupolis, north of Santorini; these suggested that Minoan civilization did, indeed, extend considerably north of Crete.

The Cousteau expedition took only a few samples of the items it encountered. Cousteau noted that his team was "frugal and careful," because "in these searches of the sea, it is important not to change the place at which an item is located; once an item is removed, it becomes difficult to date it correctly, and removal may change the character of a place, as clues to the chronology are disturbed."

Veering off his Atlantis research, Cousteau explored the wreck of the transatlantic liner *Britannic*, sister ship of the ill-fated *Titanic*. The *Britannic* sank in 1916 in the southern Aegean, having been torpedoed by a German submarine during World War I. Cousteau, whose Atlantis films are accompanied by music written for them by the Greek composer Miki Theodorakis, lowered Theodorakis inside a bathyscaphe to the unexplored British vessel.

Jacques Cousteau's main contribution to scientific and popular knowledge of this part of Aegean prehistory—and thus to the Atlantis tradition—is likely to be his depth research in Santorini and new findings around Dia. Diving around Santorini, notably in its caldera, will supplement the diggings on the island itself, particularly in Akrotiri.

Dia, as a link between Crete and Santorini, is likely to emerge as a new center of interest to Atlantis buffs—whether or not Cousteau labels his work a study of the "origins" of this "myth," or whether his findings support the view that these Minoan remnants are new proof of the accuracy of Plato's references to the civilization of Atlantis. "What was it," Cousteau mused, "we must ask ourselves, that ruined the island of Dia?" He noted that the island showed signs that it had once supported a large population, "with wooded areas, rivers, and cultivated land." Traces of asbestos furnaces, or kilns, were found.

Cousteau mentioned that one explanation of Dia's fate lies in "the explosion of the volcano at Thera (Santorini), which also affected Crete; because, as we know, the volcanic ashes from these explosions reached as far as Crete." Despite his denials that his expedition was a "search for Atlantis," Cousteau's fresh and vivid evidence is likely to support the view that the concept of Plato's Atlantis originated with the Santorini volcano eruption in the sixteenth century B.C., and that its impact destroyed a civilization of which, despite all efforts during the past half century, we still only have fragments.

Where Cousteau's search left off, the Greek Ministry of Culture and Science continues. Its Division for Undersea Exploration, established in 1976, will utilize a vessel equipped to carry out long-range submarine archaeological explorations.

CHAPTER 6

The Donnelly Version

Modern Atlantology undoubtedly would not exist—or at least would lack much of its impetus—had it not been for the efforts of a nineteenth-century Minnesota politician, Ignatius L. Donnelly. His book, *Atlantis: The Antediluvian World,* written in 1881 and published the following year by Harper and Brothers, was the first thorough synthesis of pro-Atlantean evidence. In his 500-page opus, Donnelly cited innumerable religious, mythological, folk, legendary, and scientific references to prove that Plato's lost continent was not fable, but a forgotten fact of world history.

His theses, briefly stated, were: that there was an island in the Atlantic Ocean, opposite the mouth of the Mediterranean Sea, known to the Ancients as Atlantis; that this island was the true Garden of Eden, the source of all civilization; and that in a natural disaster it sank beneath the ocean, with only a few of its inhabitants escaping by raft or boat. The tales of these survivors, he believed, endured in the form of flood and deluge legends common to almost all races and religions.

Donnelly's *Atlantis* was widely read and acclaimed; it is the basis of most subsequent research and speculation. Such writers as Lewis Spence, H. S. Bellamy, and Edgerton Sykes openly acknowledged their indebtedness to Donnelly's vast study.

Donnelly had no background as a scientist to prepare him for his undertaking. His experience was in law, poetry, oratory, and government. But he was a man of curiosity and imagination, with an ability to see connections between diverse bits of information. Ignatius Donnelly was born in Philadelphia in 1831. His father, an aspiring priest, gave up clerical training to become a physician. He contracted typhus from a patient and died when Ignatius was a small boy. His mother, a stern Irish-Catholic disciplinarian, ran a pawn shop. After her husband's death, this was the only means of support for the large family. Ignatius was a good student and distinguished himself in poetry writing. One of his poems dealing with the theme of freedom and democracy drew praise from Oliver Wendell Holmes, whom he had asked for criticism. (Donnelly's sister Eleanor later published poetry.)

After leaving high school, Donnelly became a clerk in the law offices of Benjamin Harris Brewster. He did not fit in well with the other, more genteel members of Brewster's young staff and left before completing his studies; but he apparently learned his law lessons well there and greatly admired Brewster. It was probably Brewster (who later became Attorney General of the United States) who first drew Donnelly into politics.

One of Donnelly's first political writings was an analysis by phrenology of Horace Greeley (1811–72), the controversial, combative politician-writer-publisher. Phrenology alleges that skull surface formation indicates character. Donnelly, as quoted in Martin Ridge's *Ignatius Donnelly: Portrait of a Politician*, wrote: "The characteristics common to the heads of visionary, theoretical reformers: that of largeness, fulness or overplus of brains with the front deficient in the development of those organs of judgment necessary to restrain and direct the active forces of the general intellect;—leaving to the mind its activity, its ambition, its perception, but depriving it of its practicality and its clear every day view of an every day world."

In 1854, Donnelly married Kate McCaffrey, also an Irish-Catholic Philadelphian. His mother strongly disapproved of his choice; the two women did not speak to each other for a period of 15 years. The year after his marriage, Donnelly began to involve himself slightly in local politics. His first political speech, a Fourth of July oration in favor of immigration, impressed the Philadelphia Democrats so much that they put him up for the State Legislature. But he withdrew from the race the day before the election and supported the Whig candidate.

About the same time Donnelly became involved in cooperative building association schemes. Either by intent or by accident of bad timing, Donnelly chose to move his young family westward before any of the projects were completed, and so was accused, even by his own cousin, of fraud.

Rumors were rife, at the same time, that he had mishandled money left in trust for his youngest sister. The rumors were untrue, but his embittered mother refused to quash them, with the result Donnelly's reputation in Philadelphia remained tainted.

The Ignatius Donnelly family settled in St. Paul, Minnesota, then a raw, young town enjoying an economic boom. Donnelly soon formed a partnership with John Nininger, who planned to develop a town on the west bank of the Mississippi River, 17 miles south of St. Paul. The agreement between the two was that, while Nininger and other big investors developed Nininger City, Donnelly was to use editorial and advertising means to attract immigrants to the town. To this end, he edited a German-English newspaper called the *Emigrant Aid Journal* and made several trips back east to recruit settlers and to establish an Emigrant Aid Society. Despite Donnelly's enthusiasm, the future of Nininger City looked bleak. Local elections determined that the hard-sought county seat would be placed in a rival town. When that happened, many investors began to hold onto, rather than develop, their Nininger lands, so that a highly speculative situation arose.

The gold shortage of the summer of 1857 caused eastern banks to call in western loans, local banks collapsed, and the proposed Nininger, St. Peter, and Western Railroad failed. Nininger City was bankrupt, and Donnelly's personal credit failed. Back in Philadelphia, his reputation worsened. Even locally he was considered something of a crank, but he managed to bail himself out of most of his debts and to hold on to his land.

After the crash of Nininger City, and for the rest of his life, Donnelly was always involved, peripherally or directly, with politics. He said many times that politics was a bad business, worst of all for the fellow who loses. He spoke from experience. His record was long and varied, sometimes distinguished (as Lieutenant Governor or Congressman), sometimes not (as out-of-office, backroom manipulator). He was a man of many parties, sometimes guilty of switching sides in an argument for the sake of expediency, but was usually clear on the issues of his day. Before the Civil War he was antislavery and promonopoly; afterward he was antirailroad and pro-Indian. He favored radical reconstruction of the

South, with Negro education and suffrage, universal education, with free textbooks for everyone, and conservation of the West. He was best known for his support of agricultural causes, especially paper money. He was a lively orator and a slick parliamentary manipulator.

He was out of office, it seemed, as many years as he was in, but he was always on the scene, campaigning for something or someone. During the frigid Minnesota winters, however, in an out-year, he might abandon politics to go down to his Nininger farmhouse where he would read and write and reflect long into the cold nights. It was during such a year that his interest turned to the lost continent of Atlantis.

It is not quite clear what stimulated this interest, but Donnelly had always been an avid follower of scientific developments and was widely read. Possibly, he was influenced by Jules Verne's *Twenty Thousand Leagues Under the Sea,* published in 1870. At any rate, Donnelly set out to prove some unusual theories, and in the end he achieved what was to many people a very convincing body of research and writing.

The book opens with a clear statement of purpose. Donnelly wanted to prove that, not only had there been an Atlantis, as described by Plato, where civilization had begun and spread to adjacent continents, but that it was the "true Antedeiluvian world; the Garden of Eden." The gods and goddesses of the Greeks, Phoenicians, Hindus, and Scandinavians had been simply the kings and queens of Atlantis. The sun-worshipping religions of Egypt and Peru, too, had their origins there. Since the civilization of Egypt, in particular, was a duplicate of the Atlantean, it was probably the oldest colony. Iron was first manufactured on Atlantis; the Phoenician (hence all European) and Mayan alphabets were derived from the Atlantean model; and the Aryan, or Indo-European, Semitic, and probably Turanian races originated there. Donnelly's conviction was that, as the result of an awful catastrophe, the island of Atlantis sank into the sea with nearly all its inhabitants. Those who escaped to nearby lands told stories of the disaster, which were perpetuated in flood and deluge legends.

Donnelly's theories were startling; he claimed that they "will solve many problems which now perplex mankind; they will confirm in many respects the statements in the opening chapters of Genesis; they will widen the area of human history; they will explain the remarkable resemblances which exist between the ancient civilizations found upon the opposite shores of the Atlantic Ocean, in the old and new worlds; and they will aid us to rehabilitate the fathers of our civilization, our blood, and our fundamental ideas—the men who lived, loved, and labored ages before the Aryans descended upon India, or the Phoenicians had settled in Syria, or the Goths had reached the shores of the Baltic."

The next two chapters of the book are an account of Plato's history of Atlantis, as set down in the *Timaeus* and *Critias*, and a discussion of the probabilities of Plato's story being true. Donnelly concludes that it is, for several reasons: there was nothing marvelous or improbable about the details of the Atlantean culture; if Plato had wanted simply to entertain, he would not have created so plain and reasonable a narrative. There was no evidence that Plato intended to convey a moral or political lesson; the society he described was not an ideal one. Donnelly goes on to cite physical evidence around the world which corroborates Plato's description of the island. He ends by noting that the probable reason Greeks, Romans, and most moderns set aside Plato's story as fable was that, without knowledge of the geological history of the world, they did not believe it possible that any large part of the earth's surface could have been swallowed up suddenly by the sea.

Donnelly next addresses himself to the question of whether, indeed, such a catastrophe was possible. He cites geological evidence of the day which indicated that, in the formation of the continents—and even into modern times— land masses are constantly rising and falling. To illustrate the fact that violent shifts can occur, he lists a number of earthquakes and volcanic eruptions in Iceland, Java, the Canary Islands, Thera (Santorini), Spain, Ireland, and so on. One year after the publication of Donnelly's book, the most violent eruption in recorded history occurred on the small Indonesian island of Krakatoa.

The next evidence presented by Donnelly is the discovery, made independently by several exploratory ships while mapping the bottom of the Atlantic, that there is a great elevation running the length of the ocean; in the form of such islands as the Azores, St. Paul Rocks, Ascension, and Tristan da Cunha, it reaches the surface. This, he felt, was the backbone

of the continent of Atlantis, the pathway which once extended between the continents and by means of which the plants
and animals and races of men had traveled back and forth.
He fortifies this supposition in the next chapter by citing examples of various species of animals and plants, once thought
to be found only in limited areas, which were later encountered in seemingly unlikely parts of the world. He asserts that
they all originated on Atlantis.

The next portion of the book is devoted to a survey and
comparison of the deluge legends of the world. The Bible history of the deluge as found in *Genesis* and the Chaldean
legends (both the Berrosus and the Gilgameish versions) are
treated separately. Then follow the diluvian tradition of the
Arameans, the five versions of the Indian deluge legends, the
Iranian innundation story, the three principle Greek legends
of cataclysm, and allusions to disaster in the Welsh Triads
(even though they originated as late as the twelfth or thirteenth centuries) and the Scandinavian Eddas. Donnelly attributes all similarities among them to a common folk
memory of a great disaster: the submersion of Atlantis. That
the Egyptians, as far as he could determine, had not a single
allusion to the flood was explained by him with this argument: "The Egyptians had preserved in their annals the pre-
cise history of the destruction of Atlantis ... Possessing the
real history of the local catastrophe ... they did not indulge
in any myths about a universal deluge." Because of their
great numbers, he treated the deluge legends of the Americas
and various small islands separately, but drew the same conclusions from them.

A comparison of the old and new world civilizations—in
such matters as architecture, metallurgy, sculpture, painting,
engraving, agriculture, public works, navigation, manufactures,
music, weapons, religion and religious beliefs, customs, and
games—reveals marked similarities. Donnelly thought it ab-
surd to believe that old and new worlds developed separately
or that one developed from another. Rather, they must have
sprung from a common source.

In a chapter entitled "Evidences of Intercourse with Atlantis," Donnelly pulls together myriad instances of primitive de-
pictions (on various artifacts) of animals and of races supposedly separated from them by oceans. He points to the possible Atlantean connection and asserts that all races are mix-

tures of the original Atlantean red, white, yellow, and black.

The next significant portion of the book is a detailed comparison of Atlantean lore and such civilizations as Greece, Phoenicia, Arabia, and Egypt, from the points of view of religion, commerce, art, and history. For instance: Greek mythology is really a history of the kings of Atlantis; or the extent of country covered by the commerce of the Phoenicians represents the area of the old Atlantean Empire; and so on. A similar procedure is followed with most of the peoples of the world, grouping them by race, religion, nationality, or geographical location.

The cross and the pyramid are objects of intense speculation by Donnelly. The cross, he says, symbolizes the four rivers of the Garden of Eden and, hence, of Atlantis. He points to the reverence shown to the sign in all its forms, even before Christianity. Similarly, the pyramid symbolizes the mountain that stood in the midst of Eden—and in Atlantis. Donnelly points out the similarities among all pyramids, particularly between those in Egypt and Mexico.

Donnelly makes a complex case for bronze and iron having originated in Atlantis. Though it is assumed that the Bronze Age must have been preceded by an age in which copper and tin were used separately, precious few implements made of these metals have been found anywhere in the world. For this reason, Donnelly hypothesizes that bronze smelting must have been introduced into—and not invented by—various civilizations by Atlanteans. Because Greek legends tell of earlier iron as well as bronze ages, he extends his theory to include iron.

Another subject for speculation was the comparison of Mayan (as then translated) and Phoenician alphabets, both of which, though separated by great geographical distances, were ancient, phonetic languages. He remarks that if the flood legends—in many of which sacred writings are preserved from rising waters—are worth anything, they indicate that the written word is prediluvian and, thus, Atlantean.

In one catch-all chapter, Donnelly traces many modern accoutrements to Atlantean culture. For instance, the importance and intrinsic worth of gold and silver stem from their sacredness in Atlantean religion: gold was the "tears of the sun" and silver, "the tears of the moon." He also attributes such inventions as the magnet, gunpowder, and paper to Atlantis.

Donnelly's summary chapter, a sketch of the Atlantean civilization as he perceived it, is a wistful, imaginative portrait. He concludes: "We are but beginning to understand the past: one hundred years ago the world knew nothing of Pompeii or Herculaneum; nothing of the lingual tie that binds together the Indo-European nations; nothing of the temples of Egypt; nothing of the meaning of the arrowheaded inscriptions of Babylon; nothing of the marvelous civilizations revealed in the remains of Yucatan, Mexico, and Peru. We are on the threshold. Scientific investigation is advancing with giant strides. Who shall say that one hundred years from now the great museums of the world may not be adorned with gems, statues, arms, and implements from Atlantis, while the libraries of the world shall contain translations of its inscriptions, throwing new light upon all the past history of the human race, and all the great problems which now perplex the thinkers of our day?"

As soon as the manuscript was completed, Donnelly went to New York with letters of introduction to all the major publishing houses. Expecting a rapid round of rejections, he was astounded when the first publisher he approached accepted the manuscript within 48 hours of its submission. When the book reached the bookstores the following year, he was equally amazed by the sales and by the enthusiastic reviews that appeared even in local newspapers. As a writer, he had caught the imagination of the public more successfully than he had ever done as a politician. There were a few negative reactions, mainly among academicians, who, though they grudgingly admired the great mass of materials Donnelly collected, regarded his work as illogical and unscientific. Perhaps the fairest—from the vantage point of the 1960s—description of *Atlantis: The Antediluvian World* was written decades later by one biographer, Martin Ridge, who said that he had "ransacked the works of reputable scholars such as Darwin and Fiske as well as the writings of charlatans and pseudoscientists and produced a mass of detailed material, much of it of doubtful credibility." He added:

"His carefully structured material, written in an engaging and persuasive narrative, achieved a remarkable air of authority, not only from the vast scope of his references, but also from his reliance of simple, obvious comparisons and analogies. In the use of his information, Donnelly combined common knowledge with new scientific discoveries and the works of pseudo-scientists. The style of the book, vigorous and forthright, used essentially the same rhetorical flourishes he had employed so successfully in political debate. Since *Atlantis* was basically a lawyer's brief in behalf of a speculative theory, Donnelly conformed to legal rather than scientific rules of evidence. He discarded all contradictory evidence and even distorted illustrations to prove his point. But his most serious shortcoming was in the nature of his method of analysis. Because he was not a scientist, Donnelly exercised no critical judgment of his sources whatsoever. He simply accepted at face value and quoted those authorities which presented evidence that would corroborate his hypothesis, even though they might long since have been discredited."

Donnelly could not stay out of politics for long. Two years later he ran for Congress. He lost, but soon after became involved in the formation of the Populist Party, whose activity occupied him for the rest of his life. Spurred on by the success of *Atlantis*, he wrote other books, though none of them were as well received. *Ragnorok: The Age of Fire and Gravel* attributed the deposits of clay, gravel, and silt on the earth's surface to prehistoric contact with a comet. *The Great Cryptogram* was an attempt to prove by an ingenious cipher that Francis Bacon wrote the works commonly attributed to Shakespeare. He also wrote two unsuccessful political novels. His death occurred on the first day of the twentieth century.

Donnelly's version of the Atlantis legend has had a lasting impact on the knowledge and imagination of several generations of Atlantologists. One of them, Egerton Sykes, of whose work we shall deal in later chapters, traces his lifelong interest directly to the writings of the Minnesota's Atlantean Messiah. Ignatius Donnelly was able to document and dramatize his own fascination with Atlantis with such conviction that his ideas remain fully alive in our own time.

CHAPTER 7

What Hit Atlantis?

A giant meteor, asteroid or other cosmic object hit Atlantis!

That's the answer given by some of the researchers in earth cataclysms. More cautious analysts of the fate of Atlantis see its disappearance as having taken place in various stages. Their star theorist is an Austrian, Hans Hoerbiger, who published a huge volume called *Glazialkosmogonie* (translating the title as "Cosmic Ice Theory" doesn't clarify it very much) back in 1913. World War I disrupted international cooperation, discussion of Hoerbiger's material, and the kind of scientific analysis of his concepts that might have given them wider circulation.

Hoerbiger's most striking concept is that of Lunar Capture. This means, in essence, that the moon was not a spin-off from the earth, but that it somehow came within the gravitation range of our planet—and played havoc with our geology in various stages. We now have much more data than Hoerbiger did; and we can knock a lot of his material to smithereens. But he has a tough old spokesman in Mr. Egerton Sykes, of Brighton, England, who publishes the periodical *Atlantis* as the organ of the Avalon Society and the Hoerbiger Institute.

It is fair to describe Egerton Sykes as the leading living authority on Atlantis; he was born October 9, 1894, which makes him an octogenarian. He is a sprightly, energetic, and ever-curious man, who can look back on a colorful career. He has been a member of the British diplomatic service and says that he and his wife have been in the midst of "a couple of wars, as well as five or six revolutions." He traces his family to the eleventh century and notes, "I have a full-blooded ghost in my family, who is a recorded historical character in Warwickshire."

But how did Sykes become involved with Atlantis?

He recalls that his interest began "in my earliest childhood." Sykes' mother was a friend of Helena Blavatsky, the controversial founder of Theosophy, and esoteric ideas ran in the family. He says: "I really became interested in Atlantis in 1906 when reading, in French, Jules Verne's story of the fictional visit of the Nautilus to Atlantis. But the turning point was when, while in a hospital as a soldier in World War I, I read and re-read Ignatius Donnelly." Others shared his interest, notably in France:

"After the end of the war, a society for the study of Atlantis was formed in Paris by Paul le Cour in 1926. I knew most of the founders, including the well-informed brothers René and Jean Gattefosse, with whom I corresponded until their death. The same happened with Le Cour. I was always concerned about two questions: why did Atlantis disappear and, was there any link between Then and Now?"

Egerton Sykes' researches exposed him to the rival theorists: the European "catastrophe experts," who attributed disappearance of the legendary island to cataclysmic events; and those who maintained that the earth's attraction of the moon, the "lunar capture," brought the Atlantis disaster about. He also became acquainted with the "diffusionists," who advance the concept that Atlantean population segments and cultural traditions have become diffused throughout much of the globe.

Egerton Sykes now looks back and says, "I have been firm friends with everybody who has taken a serious interest in these aspects in the past; alas, I fear I am almost the sole survivor of this group." But Sykes has passed his knowledge and enthusiasm along to a new generation of Atlantologists, almost single-handed. After World War II, he founded the Atlantis Research Center, which was first located in Rome, then in London, and now in Brighton, England, where Sykes lives. "In the process," he states with some satisfaction, "I have had the good fortune to meet everybody interested in Atlantis; and, whether I agreed with them or not, I have printed their ideas in my two periodicals, *Atlantis* or *New World Antiquity*."

While Sykes' interest in Atlantis has not flagged, he did publish a journal of radiesthesia for 16 years, which he discontinued "for lack of time," and another one dealing with Unidentified Flying Objects, which he gave up as he got "bored with UFOs, because they seemed so futile." Yet, Sykes is not easily bored. He and his wife, as he puts it, have "thoroughly enjoyed life and a fifty-nine-year companionship." They are heavily involved in British politics. In his life, Sykes feels, there has "never been a dull moment," as he has been an engineer, diplomat, journalist, and soldier; he knows French, German, and Polish with such fluency that he has made broadcasts in all three languages, as well as English.

Sykes and I crossed the Atlantic Ocean, in opposite directions, in the summer of 1976. Sykes was on his way to a California conference (dealing with the subject of Atlantis, of course), while I was on my way from New York to Greece (to study the latest findings in marine archaeology, on Atlantis, of course). "I'm good for another 15 years yet," the sprightly opinionated octogenarian said to me. "After all, I'm the last of the Atlantologists of the Old School, and you won't find the likes of me again." Sykes, researcher into the Atlantis legend, is something of an elusive legend himself—a former member of the British foreign service, and evasive when it comes to pinning down the basis of his passionate interest in the Lost Continent.

Sykes is a walking encyclopedia of Atlantis lore and fact, an international one-man clearing house always in danger of being overwhelmed by piles of books, pamphlets, and worldwide correspondence. He is working on a definitive book on his research and conclusions, and I, for one, can hardly wait to read it. Meanwhile, on the pages of his *Atlantis* periodical, Egerton Sykes has put down some of his ideas, and they do not lack verve, iconoclasm, or a no-nonsense self-assurance.

I was frankly overwhelmed by the definitive style Sykes used in a two-part presentation "Atlantis: a New Concept," which appeared in his periodical's issues for May–June and July–August 1974. In it, Sykes gave the names of major cities of Atlantis, described Atlantean temples and their rites—in other words, provided detail that called for documentation that would, to say the least, be extremely hard to obtain. Sykes said that his work was made possible because "the Tuatha left us a number of records which have told us not only their names for four of the Cities of Atlantis, out of a total of seven of which tradition tells us." He added that he also obtained "records of the Treasures of the various Temples plus some details as to what happened to them."

Who, I asked Sykes, were the Tuatha? His answer was that they were ancient Irish tribes, going back to pre-Vedic times—the period of prehistoric India that produced the subcontinent's richest religio-philosophic traditions. Without further detailed attribution, Egerton Sykes then gives names to the gods and goddesses of Atlantis that are familiar from Egyptian-Hellenic traditions. This oddity makes sense, of course, if one assumes that the refugees from Atlantis selected, among other regions, the Eastern Mediterranean and brought not only their mythology, practices, and traditions, with them, but the very names of their divinities as well. Scattering in many directions, they could also have transmitted similar ideas to the island that is today's Ireland.

As Sykes put it, it was about 9500 B.C. that Atlantis "sank beneath the waves and it was at that juncture that the links joining Atlantis to the culture of the present day were forged." I think we must simply accept Sykes' account for what it is: the sum total of knowledge an extremely devoted and erudite man has assembled. It would take an international committee of nit-pickers to argue each point with him.

Egerton Sykes has collected Atlantean data from around the world which suggests to him Atlantis formed an S-shaped continent that curved parallel with the African coast. We can look at the map and see the ridge that stretches from the Azores to Ascension Island. The maps that now show the submarine territory of Atlantic Ocean indicate a central ridge, "its mountainous backbone."

But back to the question we asked at the beginning of this chapter: What hit Atlantis?

Sykes' answer is unequivocal: "The cause of its destruction was a meteor strike of an extensive nature in the region of the Caribbean and the Carolina coast, where there are numerous meteor craters, both large and small, showing the magnitude of the disaster." He gives us this picture of the chronology of events: "A series of meteorites ranging from half a mile in diameter down to a few yards fell almost simultaneously, and the combined shock waves caused the whole of the Dolphin Ridge to drop, leaving only major peaks above water," these being the Azores and Ascension Island, referred to above. According to Sykes, Madeira, the Canaries, and the Cape Verde Islands and Bimini, off the

Florida coast, also survived, "although physically not connected with the Atlantis island."

While "the toll of human life was enormous," Sykes states
"certain small groups managed to escape," thanks to "their
professions and their situations." These privileged displaced
persons were of three main categories: the priestesses of
Atlantis, who became the Amazons; the temple functionaries,
who became the Tuatha of Ireland; and, finally, the military
guards, of whom Mr. Sykes states that they became "the
Aesir."

Looking at the islands that are scattered through the Atlantic Ocean and the Caribbean, Sykes finds that there—and
wherever else Atlantean and post-Atlantean civilizations were
established—traces may still be observed. As he puts it, "now,
thousands of years later, various of the Treasures have managed to survive, some by design, others by accident." He
adds that it "has now been possible to site four of the seven
Cities of Atlantis with their attendant Temples as also one
other city with its Temple." How was this done? Over a
period of 25 years, Sykes says, lists of sacred Treasures of
the Tuatha, the Celts, and the Aesir were drawn up, and
from these Atlantean origins were deduced. The names of
the cities, according to this account, "are those given by the
Tuatha and others, and they may well have had completely
different names in the time of Atlantis."

Sykes puts strong emphasis on "continuity of occupation"
of these cities in some form or another, from the days of
Atlantis "until the present day." Seven cities, then, are supposed to have existed, and three of them would thus have to
be submerged, awaiting sophisticated underwater exploration.
He places the city he calls Falias at the center of a complex
consisting of two islands of the Azores groups, San Miguel
and Santa Maria. Citing Tuatha sources, he says that Falias
was known as the City with the Golden Gates, while "to the
Atlanteans it may have had a name linked with the Temple of
Poseidon, of which the Golden Gates formed the entrance;
its remains now lie a few miles to the southeast."

Poseidon, of course, was the god of the waters in Greek
mythology; but much of all ancient mythology, to Atlantologists, is based on Atlantis traditions, anyway. Sykes adds
these intriguing details: "An Egyptian Temple stood on the
West of Santa Maria, near the village of Miau Miau named

after the Temple to Bast, the Cat Goddess, which once stood there. In its penetralia was kept the 'Stone of Death, Crowned with Pale Fire,' salvaged from the Temple with the Golden Gates. Perhaps the most important artifact to come from Atlantis down to our own times. Originally a Meteorite, it ended up as the Throne of Britain."

Sykes says that the collapse of Atlantis was survived by only those inhabitants of Falias who were visiting the Temple or, a second outstanding edifice, the Nunnery or College of San Miguel. Only the Amazon priestesses, he writes, were able "to continue in residence." They were cut off for some time, but later established contact with other surviving centers of Atlantean civilization. As an aside, Egerton Sykes notes that this particular temple had a music teaching specialty, including singing, and "Calypso music having been invented here named after an early High Priestess."

If that is so, undersea explorer Jacques Cousteau has named his famous vessel, *The Calypso*, after an Atlantean goddess—which would seem to be a good omen for his efforts to trace Atlantis remains in the Thera–Crete area of the Mediterranean. Raiders preyed on the isolated Atlantean cities, we are told, and "one of the successful raiding expeditions was that of the Tuirenn Brothers," coming from what is now Ireland, who visited all four cities. From Falias "they brought the Stone of Death, by then transmuted into the Stone of Destiny." Sykes says that "on its arrival in Ireland," the stone "became the Throne of Tara which cried out if an imposter sat on it."

Another visitor, or marauder, was Pepi the First of Egypt who, Sykes believes, "sent out exploring teams to the Atlantic Islands" about 2800 B.C. By this time the local temple had turned from devotion to Poseidon to that of the cat goddess. Sykes quotes an historian, Thevet, who visited San Miguel in 1675 as describing a cave on the north side of the island, "in which were two stone stelae / pillars of vertical slabs of stone / bearing inscriptions which he thought were in Hebrew. He said the cave had to be sealed because 'several visitors had died from fumes from the adjoining volcanic craters and thermal springs.'"

According to this survey, the "Amazon Sisterhood" of Atlantis "managed not only to maintain their hold on the off-shore islands"—of the shore of North Africa, one assumes—

"adjacent to their Temples but also to dominate the coast line from Thymaterium-Mogador in the North, to Kerne, in the South, opposite the Cap Verde Islands, which today remain a Portuguese possession." Rather quickly, Sykes passes over a wide historical and geographic range when he adds: "Inland they penetrated as far East as Nysa—The City of Brass in the Hoggar, while on the Mediterranean they had an island fastness called Kakhale or Horse Head. Later, it became Carthage. In the background was the knowledge of the entire Classical World that the Temple Cities of Gorias and Finias, not to speak of Falias and Murias, housed Treasures of infinite value. One of these was the Diadem or Girdle of State of the Amazon Queens (kept in Gorias, but removed for saftey at the time of an attack by the Heraclibae), which was in existence until 1942, and of which photographs have been taken."

Sykes places the Temple of Gorias on "what is now the Gran Curral of Madeira, adjoining the orange groves where grow the Golden Apples of the Sun." Attacks on these various cities or city-states, with varying success, are recorded. The report states that "the only people able to establish footholds on the Gorias or Finias were the Egyptians and Carthagenians, who alternated possession over long periods of time. Temples of Bast and Isis, Tantith and Selene, abounded. After the fall of Carthage, the Romans left them undisturbed. The great change occurred in 1111 A.D. when Muslim hordes invaded and killed or enslaved the whole population, leaving them arid wastes."

In his description of the city of Finias, Sykes notes that its temple contained the so-called Chariot of the Gods, which had been "one of the Wonders of the Atlantean World," a full-sized replica of the chariot of Poseidon, complete with horses and drivers, made of solid gold. "On ceremonial occasions," he says, "it was taken out and paraded through the streets." It was known to both Hanno and Alexander the Great. He adds that Finias was a metal-working center, that horses and dogs were bred by the inhabitants and that it supplied "many sorts of domestic wares." As for the golden Chariot of the Gods—various invaders may have tried to abscond with it, but Mr. Sykes thinks it is "probably lying somewhere in the sea between Lanzarotte and Teneriffe."

We shall deal with recent underwater research around the

Caribbean island of Bimini in a later chapter. But Egerton Sykes has come to the conclusion that this spot, and specifically its town-center and Temple of Murias has a long Atlantean tradition. He feels that the temple survived the cataclysm that submerged Atlantis, mainly because it stood on a hill, whereas the parent city of Murias was located in a valley that is now somewhere beneath the Caribbean sea between Bimini and one of the islands of the Bahamas group.

Sykes says that the whole region, including the relatively large island of Andros in the Bahamas, was a complex of the Bimini Temple and its "ancillary buildings such as clinics, schools, dwelling houses for the staff and barracks for the troops." The Bimini Temple, he writes, "had windows of crystal, which was translucent rather than transparent," because plate glass had not yet been invented. The famous Crystal Skull found in the area, carved from a single piece of rock crystal, is a magnificent example of an era of high artistry, whatever its specific name or origin.

Sykes' enthusiasm is catching. He believes that the Temple of Bimini was, in one way or another, "in continuous use until the beginning of our Era." Ponce de Leon, he says, made a mistake when he landed in Florida—he had actually been looking for the "Fountain of Youth" on Bimini; he also thinks that Miami originally got its name from the Atlantean-Egyptian Cat Temple's name, Miau-Miau (or Miaw-Miaw), which accepts the Miami tribe of Indians of the Algonquin linguistic stock as being related to the Egyptian period rather than the Atlantean. He mentions that there is a connecting link of serpent worship from the West Indies to the north, still under investigation.

Sykes concludes that final sinking of the Temple of Bimini took place before the beginning of our Era, after having been "in constant use by one sect or another until then." He feels that the lowering of the Continental Shelf was "probably a gradual process which eventually prevented the building from being used." Like the rest of the temples of Atlantis, he points out, the one on Bimini had many functions that made it a seat of government, a hospital, a home for travelers in distress, as well as a shipyard with repair facilities." Sykes regards Atlantean temples as having been "as solid a building as any modern church or cathedral, but without roofs, the arch not having been invented," having been produced just like them, with "manual labor, plus a lot of skilled thought in the lay-out."

The mysteries which men like Mr. Sykes explore in their search for the truth about Atlantis inevitably yield unexpected puzzles on the way. Among the more fascinating and elusive of these is that of an alleged testament by the great amateur archaeologist, Heinrich Schliemann, which suggested that he had sought and found Atlantis; it is the next target of our inquiry.

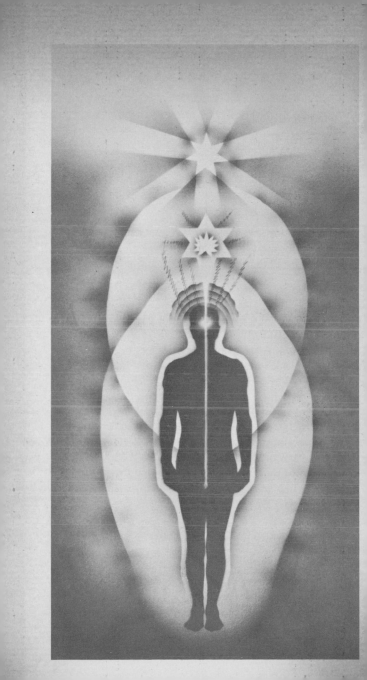

Astara

792 West Arrow Highway
Upland, Calif. 91786

CHAPTER 8

The Great Schliemann Mystery

The underwater explorations for remnants of Atlantis in the Bimini area and off the Atlantic coast of Spain have drawn on psychic, intuitive, and other extrasensory impressions or memories of Atlantis. Inevitably, those who today utilize the work of psychics in archaeology—the way dowsing is used to find underground water—recall the phenomenal achievement of the self-educated German archaeologist Heinrich Schliemann (1822–1890), who excavated the ancient Greek city of Troy; Schliemann, according to this view, at least unconsciously used psychic powers to locate Troy, and submarine evidence of Atlantis might therefore be located in a similar manner. Today's leading pioneer in "intuitive" archaeology is Dr. J. Norman Emerson, Professor of Archaeology and Anthropology, University of Toronto.

The Bimini searches, in particular, relied not only on Edgar Cayce's references to the area as containing remnants of Atlantis, but on the help of participants who sought to utilize clairvoyant powers to narrow down the explorations' target. Schliemann's example is a fitting inspiration for daring amateur and professional archaeologists. He described in candid detail how even as a very small boy, he was enthralled by folkloric tales, in the little town of Ankershagen, that spoke of buried treasure and dramatic legends, of past violence and deaths. When he received a history book for his eighth birthday, Heinrich argued with his father about a drawing of Troy, saying, "Daddy, if it had such enormous walls, it can't just have disappeared but must still be hidden under the dust and ruins of centuries."

Schliemann was obsessed with Troy and ancient Greece; reincarnationists could easily explain his single-mindedness in terms that fit their doctrine: Heinrich Schliemann must have been a resident of Troy in an earlier incarnation, and his overriding drive to rediscover the ancient city was based on memories of an earlier life. Closely related to this concept is the hypothesis that Schliemann was aided by clairvoyant powers in locating Troy, contrary to the opinions of professional archaeologists.

It is quite true that Schliemann had a mystic streak. He describes his vivid premonition of a fire that destroyed the city of Memel. Omens and hunches played a large part in the varied career of this man who managed to be commercially successful, a linguist of awesome capacity, and, of course, a daring archaeologist. That today's Atlantis searchers find Schliemann's example inspiring is hardly surprising.

An unsolved mystery linking Schliemann's name to the Atlantis legend was brought to public attention by Egerton Sykes: more than two decades after the German archaeologist's death, on October 20, 1912. An article entitled, "How I Found the Lost Atlantis," appeared in the New York *American*, a daily paper owned by William Randolph Hearst. The article carried the byline of Dr. Paul Schliemann, identified as a grandson of the great archaeologist. The article alleged that Heinrich Schliemann, a few days before his death in Naples, gave a sealed envelope to a friend marked, "To be opened only by a member of my family who solemnly vows to devote his whole life to the researches outlined therein." The article also claimed that, on his deathbed, Schliemann had called for a pencil and paper in order to write the following separate message:

"Confidential addition to the sealed envelope: Break the owl-headed vase. Pay attention to the contents. It concerns Atlantis. Investigate the east of the ruins of the Temple of Sais and the Cemetery of the Chacúna Valley. Important. It proves the system. Night approaches. Goodbye."

Schliemann's grandson, Paul—if, indeed, he was the author of this sensational article—decided after years of world travel to act for his family, retrieve the letter from a French bank, open the envelope, and publicize its contents. According to this account, Heinrich Schliemann left a 19-point testament of documentation and hypotheses (the italic interpolations are by Mr. Sykes, who published the text in his periodical *Atlantis*, Vol. 4, No. 5, January 1952) as follows:

(1) "I have come to the conclusion that the Lost Atlantis was not only a great territory between America and the West Coast of Africa and Europe, but the cradle of our civilisation, as well. There has been much dispute amongst scientists in this matter. According to one group, the tradition of Atlantis is purely fiction founded upon fragmentary accounts of a deluge some thousand of years before the Christian era. Others declare the tradition wholly historical, but incapable of absolute proof.

(2) "In the included material, records are to be found, the proofs which exist in my mind of the matter. Whoever takes the charge of this mission, is solemnly obligated to continue my researches, and to form a definite statement, using as well the matter I leave with this, and crediting me with my just dues in the discovery. A special fund is deposited in the Bank of France to be paid to the bearer of the enclosed receipt, and this should pay the expenses of the research. The Almighty be with this great effort.

(3) "When in 1875 I made the excavation of the ruins of Troy at Hissarlik, and discovered in the second city the famous Treasure of Priam, I found among that treasure, a peculiar bronze vase of great size. Within it were several pieces of pottery, various small images of peculiar metal, coins of the same metal, and objects made out of fossilised bone. Some of these objects, and the bronze vase, were engraved with a sentence in Phoenician hieroglyphics. The sentence read: From the King Chronos of Atlantis.

(4) "You who read can imagine my excitement! Here was the first, the very first, material evidence of that great continent, whose legend had lived for ages throughout the world. This material I kept secret, eager to make it the basis of investigations, which I felt would prove of infinitely more importance than the discovery of a hundred Troys.

(5) "In 1883, I found in the Louvre, a collection of objects excavated from Tiahunaca in Central America—(*This was obviously a misprint, either it should have been Tiahunaca in South America, or Teohuatican in Central America. If the first is correct it would provide the earliest suggested link between the Lake Titicaca culture and Atlantis.*) Among these I discovered pieces of pottery of exactly the same shape and material, and objects of fossilised bone which reproduced, line for line, those which I had found in the bronze vase of the

Treasure of Priam! The similarity could not be a coincidence. The shape and decorations were too simple for that. It is beyond the range of coincidence for two artists in such widely separated countries as Central America and Crete—(*An obvious misprint for Asia Minor, and one which appears to have passed unnoticed by those critics of the story who seized on the first one*)—to make two vases, and I mention only one of the objects, of exactly the same shape, the same size, and with curious owl's heads arranged the same way on each.

(6) "The Central American Vases had no Phoenician characters upon them, nor writing of any sort. I hurried away to examine my own objects, and by tests and exhaustive examinations became convinced that the inscriptions had been made by other hands after the objects themselves had been manufactured.

(7) "I secured pieces of these simulacrums from Tiahuanaca—(*Here the same observations as before regarding misprints applies*)—and subjected them to chemical and microscopic analysis. These tests proved conclusively that both the Central American vases, and those from Troy, had been made from the same peculiar clay, and, I learned later, further and definitely, that this clay does *not* exist either in old Phoenicia, nor in Central America.

(8) "The metal objects I had analysed because I could not recognize what they were made of. The metal was unlike any I have ever seen. The chemical analysis showed the material to be platinum, aluminium and copper—a combination never before found in the remains of the ancients and unknown today.

(9) "Objects then, perfectly similar and having unquestionably a common source, were found in such widely separated countries as these. The objects themselves are not Phoenician, Mycenean, nor Central American. What is the conclusion? That they came to both places from a common centre. The inscription on the objects gave that centre—it was Atlantis.

(10) "That the objects were held in great veneration is shown from their presence among the Treasure of Priam, and the special receptacle which held them. Their character left me no doubt that they were objects of sacred ceremonies, and from the same temple.

(11) "This extraordinary discovery, and my failing health, induced me to push more rapidly my investigations. I found

in the Museum at St. Petersburg, one of the oldest papyrus rolls in existence. It was written in the reign of Pharaoh Sent (Senedi) in the Second Dynasty, or 4,571 B.C. It contained a description of how the Pharaoh named, sent out an expedition 'to the West' in search of the traces of the Land of Atlantis whence 3,350 years ago the ancestors of the Egyptians arrived carrying with themselves all the wisdom of their native lands. Another papyrus in the same museum written by Manetho, refers to a period of 13,900 years as the reign of the sages of Atlantis. This papyrus places this at the beginnings of Egyptian history; it approximates 16,000 years ago.

(12) "An inscription which I excavated at the Lion Gate at Mycenae in Crete (*this should read Greece*) recites that Misor, from whom, according to the inscription, the Egyptians were descended, was the child of Taaut or Thoth, the God of History, and that Taaut was the emigrated son of a 'Priest of Atlantis', who, having fallen in love with a daughter of King Chronos, escaped and landed after many wanderings in Egypt. He built the first temple at Sais, and there taught the widsom of his native land. This full inscription is most important and I have kept it secret. You will find it among the papers.

(13) "One of the tables of my Trojan excavations gives also a medical treatise of the Egyptian priests—for there was communication between Crete (*read Asia Minor*) and Egypt for many centuries—for the removal of a cataract from the eye, and an ulcer from the intestines, by means of surgery. I have read almost a similar formula in a Spanish manuscript in Berlin, whose writer took it from an Aztec priest in Mexico. That priest had gotten it from an ancient Mayan manuscript.

(14) "In coming to my conclusions, I must say that neither the Egyptians nor the Mayan race that made the civilisation of Central America were great navigators. They had no ships to cross the Atlantic. Nor did they. We can dismiss the agency of the Phoenicians as a real link between the two hemispheres. Yet the similarity of Egyptian and Mayan life and civilisation is so perfect that it is impossible to think of it as an accident. We find no such accidents in nature or history. The only possibility is that there was, as the legend says, a great continent that connected what we now call the New World with what we call the Old. Perhaps at this time what

there was of Europe and America, was populated with monsters. Africa possibly had a monkey-like negro race. Man, in our sense, had not overrun them. But there was a land where civilisation as high as that we now know and perhaps even higher, was flourishing. Its outskirts were the edge of the wilderness. It was Atlantis. From Atlantis came colonies that settled in Egypt and Central America.

(15) "The religion of Egypt was pre-eminently Sun Worship. Ra was the Sun God of the Egyptians. The religion of the Mayas of Central America was the same. Ra-Na was the God of the ancient Peruvians.

(16) "My long archaeological studies of various nations have proven all of them to show traces of their earliest childhood and maturity. But I have failed to find any trace of a rude and savage Egypt, or a rude barbarous Maya race. I have found both these nations mature in their very earliest period, skilful, strong and learned. I never have found a time when they lacked the ability to organize their labour, nor lacking in ability to dig canals, build highways, pyramids and temples, to irrigate fields, nor a time when they did not know medicine, astronomy, and the principles of highly organized government. Like the Mayas, the Egyptians practised monogamy, and they built their cities and temples in the same style, exhibiting a technical knowledge and skill that remains a puzzle to the engineers of this age. Neither Egyptians nor Mayas were a black race, but yellow. Both nations had slaves and an intellectual class, but the relations between the classes were cordial and humane. Their basic principles of government were the same.

(17) "Lepsius found the same sacred symbols in the ceremonials of the Egyptians as in the Peruvians. Le Plongeon, the great French archaeologist (*le Plongeon was an American citizen at the close of his life, but of French descent*) recovered in Chichen-Itza in Yutacan, the figure of a god, who was club-footed, and who bore in every way the attributes of the great god Thoth of the Egyptians.

(18) "In the Egyptian and the American pyramids, the outside was covered with a thick coating of smooth and shining cement of such strength as our builders are unable to get. [Alexander von] Humboldt [German explorer in Central and South America, 1769–1859] considered the pyramid of

Choula to be of the same type as the Temple of Jupiter at Belus.

(19) "In both America and Egypt, the pyramids were built in the same style. I have found the pyramids on both sides of the Atlantic with their four sides pointing astronomically like the arms of the cross, in the same directions. In both, the line through the centre is in the astronomical meridian. The construction in grades and steps is the same, and in both cases the larger pyramids are dedicated to the Sun."

So much for Heinrich Schliemann's alleged Atlantis "testament." What, looking back over more than half a century, are we to make of this remarkable, but distinctly odd, piece of writing? Considering its source, and the lack of further documentation during the intervening period, the whole thing reads like a hoax. Egerton Sykes, in addition to the interpolation he made in publishing the text, raised a number of questions that dealt wtih the appearance and substance of the article. A collaborator of Schliemann, Wilhelm Dörpfeld, commented on the matter in a letter to Alexander Bessmertny, who published it in his book, *Atlantis*. Dörpfeld said, "To my knowledge, Heinrich Schliemann never occupied himself in any deep manner in the question of Atlantis. At least, I never heard any allusion to work of this kind, although I was his collaborator from 1882 until his death in 1890. But Schliemann spoke sometimes on the question of Atlantis, and I consider it possible that he may have put together some notes relating to this question." Dörpfeld doubted "the existence of an original work of his on this theme."

Sykes expressed puzzlement about the disjointed and incomplete nature of researches allegedly undertaken by Paul Schliemann after he read his grandfather's Atlantis testament. According to the article, reprinted in the British Sunday paper *Weekly Budget* (November 17, 1912), Paul sought to document Heinrich Schliemann's ideas at first hand. Among his grandfather's collection he found an owl-headed vase, broke it, and found a white metal square covered with drawings of figures and, in Phoenician script, the words "Issued in the Temple of the Transparent Walls." He assumed that, as the medal could not have been squeezed through the narrow neck of the vase, Heinrich Schliemann must have had other vases bearing different inscriptions. According to the article, Paul toured Mexico, other areas of Central America, and Peru. He found owl-headed vases in a cemetery of the Chucuna Valley, without medals, but with supposedly "startling" inscriptions. The pyramid of Teotihuacán yielded medals without inscriptions. Sykes suggested these medals were "token receipts for votive offerings."

Paul Schliemann asserted he found "clear indications of the site of the City of the Golden Gates, and two clear references to the Temple of Transparent Walls." He wondered whether the word "transparent" had only "symbolic meaning, or did there really exist a structure with transparent walls"? He did not know the answer to this question but alleged he could "prove" the Phoenicians had received their knowledge of glass-making from the "People who lived beyond the Pillars of Hercules." The article concluded with what Sykes described as "two of the most disputed texts in the whole history of Atlantean Research," the so-called Troano Codex which referred to destruction, by earthquakes, of "the Land of Mu" and an inscription said to have been discovered on the walls of a Temple in Lhasa, Tibet, written in 2000 B.C. in the Chaldean language; it said:

"When the star Bal fell on the place where is now only sea and sky, the Seven Cities with the Golden Gates and their Transparent Temples quivered and shook like the leaves of a tree in a storm. And behold a flood of smoke and fire arose from the palaces. Agony and cries of the multitude filled the air. They sought refuge in their temples and cities. And the wise Mu, the hieratic of Ra-Mu, arose and said unto them: 'Did I not predict all this?' And the women, and the men, in their precious stones and shining garments, lamented, 'Mu, save us!' and Mu replied, 'You shall die, together with your slaves and your riches, and from your ashes shall arise new nations. If they forget they are superior, not because of what they put on, but, because of what they put out, the same lot shall befall them.' Flame and smoke choked the words of Mu. The land and its inhabitants were torn to pieces and swallowed by the depths in a few months."

Sykes, trying to be fair in the face of doubtful documentation, noted the "uncertainty about Mu," an abbreviation of Lemuria, a legendary sunken continent in the Pacific or Indian Oceans. The term "Lemuria" was first used by Philip L. Slater, a naturalist, because of the supposed presence of "lemurs" on the continent's territory. Today, the lemur is a nocturnal mammal found mainly in Madagascar; lemurs, distantly related to the monkey family, are treated by naturalists as a distinctive group, Lemuroidea.

If Slater invented the term "Lemuria", and if Mu (or, Moo) derived from it, how could the word appear in the Troano Codex, said to be written in 1550, or in an ancient Tibetan inscription? Sykes notes that "it is not possible" to trace the use of the word "Mu" prior to the nineteenth century, but added that "this does not preclude its existence." And what had Mu to do with Schliemann's search for Atlantis? I think most Atlantologists would agree with Sykes that "no matter what may have happened in the past, the use of the name Mu should be restricted to the Pacific area"—although, as we note in our chapter on Hawaii, Kahuna traditions include the possible settlement of this Pacific island group by men and women descended from Atlantis. Sykes attributed the uniform style in which varied texts appear in the Paul Schliemann article to the likelihood that all of them were translated by one person. He attributed errors of fact to "bad editing and proof reading."

Egerton Sykes, tolerant of the alleged Schliemann article as a whole, commented that "although the statements are sensational, they carry conviction," but added that "it is difficult to understand why in the intervening years we have neither confirmation nor refutation from the lawyers, bankers and others involved in the execution of the will of Heinrich Schliemann." Sykes suggested that "it is the complete absence of negative evidence that tends to confirm the accuracy of the story."

But what about Dr. Paul Schliemann himself? Again, the solitary efforts of Sykes have provided us with the relatively scant biographical facts. A British explorer, Mitchell Hedges, who found the famous Crystal Skull in the Caribbean, is quoted by Sykes as having known young Schliemann in New York, where he lived on a small yacht berthed in the city's harbor. Paul Schliemann is said to have disappeared during World War I to join the German army and to have died during the war. Sykes calculates that, on the basis of biographical information given in the New York *American*, he must have been about twenty-eight years old when the article appeared.

Egerton Sykes, for all his caution concerning the 1912 article, credits Paul Schliemann with "the first references to the Temple of the Crystal Walls and the City of the Golden Gates, the first being in Bimini and the second adjacent to Santa Maria in the Azores." He also notes that young Schliemann "introduced the factor of the Owl-Headed Vases which are encountered on both sides of the Atlantic." He concluded that while Paul Schliemann "may not have been right in his conclusions," he "certainly provided an impetus to Atlantean research."

But the likelihood still remains that the man who supplied such "impetus" possibly never existed. The multitalented, hard-driving financier-archaeologist Heinrich Schliemann married twice, first in Russia and later in Greece. The first marriage, in St. Petersburg to Catharine, lasted from 1852 to 1868. While the marital venture was unsatisfactory from the beginning, it produced one son, Sergius or Serge, born in 1855, and two daughters, Nadya and Natalie. The Schliemanns finally divorced while Heinrich resided in Indianapolis, Indiana. From there he corresponded with the Archbishop of Greece, asking for a suitable Hellenic mate; ultimately, on September 24, 1869, he married the 17-year-old Sophia Engastromenos (Schliemann was then 47); they had a son, Agamemnon, born in 1871 and a daughter, Andromache, born in 1878.

Sykes writes that the mysterious Paul Schliemann was married to a woman who later became the wife of a leading Greek statesman; this is an error: it was Agamemnon Schliemann who married a young actress, Nadine, whose second husband was the one-time Premier Constantine Tsaldaris; I had several opportunities to meet Mr. and Mrs. Tsaldaris in Athens during the statesman's premiership in the late 1940s and early 1950s.

As Agamemnon and Nadine Schliemann divorced after a childless marriage, the Greek Schliemann line ended with Agamemnon in the country that had absorbed Heinrich Schliemann's passionate attention during the most creative part of his life. Did Sergius Schliemann, the Russian son of Heinrich, have a son named Paul? Leading biographers, such as the Germans Ernst Meyer and Emil Ludwig, make no reference to such offspring. The files of the German Archaeological Institute in Athens, and the even more extensive archives of its equivalent in Rome, contain no references to writings by a Paul Schliemann. I contacted Greek historians of the archaeological field in Athens in the summer of 1976, and they were unable to corroborate the hypothesis of Paul's existence. Meyer's collection of Heinrich Schliemann's letters, with an introduction by Schliemann's archaeological collaborator Wilhelm Dörpfeld, contain no reference to such a grandson, nor, for that matter, to Atlantis.

Heinrich Schliemann's first marriage, to Catharine, led to such alienation and recrimination that Heinrich even forbade Sergius to write him letters in the Russian language; the break with his Russian wife and children was near-total. The leading Schliemann authority in modern Greece is Professor George Korres, a member of the Philosophical Faculty of Athens University. Backed by detailed files and meticulous research into Heinrich Schliemann's life and work, Professor Korres today says, "I have heard the name of Paul Schliemann spoken, but only in most ephemeral terms. There are no birth or death records concerning such a man, no letters by him or referring to him of which I am aware. I frankly doubt that he existed."

Despite the conflict of evidence, Sykes is certain that Paul Schliemann actually did exist. He has a friend, still alive, who knew him in person and believes that he would use the name "Paul" rather than "Agamemnon" while in the States. Sykes continues to assume that Paul Schliemann appears to have died in the German army during the First World War.

Sykes agrees that the alternative view that he might have been the son of Sergius would explain his knowledge of Russian sources. The interesting point is that he and his yacht vanished within a week or so of the article being published.

Sykes observes that the information about the marriage to Nadine came from France about the time of Bessmertny. All records were lost when Poland was invaded in 1939.

Wherever he may have been born, Sykes says, most Soviet sources treat him as a German.

The only remaining descendent of Heinrich Schliemann in Greece today is Mrs. Lilian Melas, the sprightly white-haired widow of Schliemann's grandson Leno, an architect who died in the 1960's. Mrs. Melas told me that she "surely would have known" of Paul Schliemann if such a grandson had existed and suggested that he was a "*personage imaginaire* in the family's genealogy."

Atlantis and Paul Schliemann prove to be equally elusive.

CHAPTER 9

Did a Huge Meteor
Destroy Atlantis?

The successful archaeological studies in Greece's Aegean Sea
have drawn public attention away from other hypotheses
concerning the cataclysm which may have destroyed Atlantis.
As noted earlier, one of these concepts attributes the legendary island's end to the impact of one or several huge meteors.
Hoerbiger, the Austrian authority on this subject, and the as-
sociations that carry on the research he began point to several
enormous craters that may have been created by meteors of
the type that destroyed Atlantis, either in stages or in a single
cataclysm.

An examination of craters on the surface of the earth may
also offer clues to craters yet to be located beneath the
oceans; possibly, at the bottom of the sea and now covered
with the debris of millennia, are enormous craters which
have, so far, eluded undersea searches. Perhaps sophisticated
deep-sea diving facilities such as those employed by the well-
known French underwater explorer Jacques Cousteau—who
examined the Aegean Sea in 1975 and 1976—would be needed to find and analyze such craters.

A "crater", according to *Webster's New World Dictionary*,
is: the bowl-shaped cavity at the mouth of a volcano; and, a
pit, as one made by a bomb explosion. Broadly defined, a
crater is any pit-like cavity formed in solid matter by spon-
taneous natural action or by induced force. Craters can range
in size from a fraction of an inch to many miles in diameter.
In each case, however, displacement of matter has occurred
in the formation of the crater.

Oddly, while two major craters of this type exist in the
United States, neither as tourist attractions nor as centers of
mystical speculations have these spots captured the public's
imagination. They are: the Great Meteor Crater in Arizona

(also known as the "Barringer Crater," after Daniel Moreau Barringer, a Philadelphia mining engineer who became fascinated by this phenomenon in 1902), and Crater Lake in southern Oregon, which fills the crater of an extinct volcano, surrounded by 2,000-foot-high lava cliffs. Paradoxically, Crater Lake gained its greatest national publicity in recent years when, in 1975, visitors to the park suffered from a minor food poisoning epidemic: the area had to be closed off and a minor panic among families who had visited the lake made nationwide headlines.

The Barringer Crater of Arizona has not experienced either positive or negative publicity in recent years, although it is an awesome sight—a gigantic mouth yawning in the midst of a vast and barren plain. Located in the northeastern part of the state, off Highway 66, east of Flagstaff, the crater's terrain has served as a training site for space-traveling astronauts. The development of specialists in ground conditions of space territory, known as astrogeologists, has kept pace with the explorations of the Moon and Mars. Astrogeologists regard Arizona's Meteor Crater as an excellent example of the earth's meteoritic craters. Its grounds are in many ways similar to the crater-pocked surface of the moon and, as photographed in 1976, Mars as well.

Even before lunar explorations captured the public's imagination, the territory of the Barrington Crater gave astronauts a chance to simulate their moon walks before they took their trips into space. Unlike many other craters on earth, which have filled up with water and have been altered by erosion or simply disappeared due to shifting sands or other natural phenomena, Meteor Crater remains virtually unchanged by winds, waters, or time.

Simply described, it is a bowl-shaped pit in the high desert floor. Meteor Crater looks like the top of an extinct volcano. No flora or fauna, unless microscopic in size, can be seen growing in or near the crater. The earth is grayish-brown inside the crater and all around it. East of the crater, the Petrified Forest contains many acres of fragmentary trees—now turned to agate—which bloomed some 160 million years ago. Surrounding the crater and stretching northwest are buttes, cones, and volcanic ash residue of the Painted Desert.

Soil samples taken from the floor of Meteor Crater have yielded bits of shell and other debris left from a long-past era—an age when waters covered the desert floor and our own continent may have been submerged, at least in part, beneath the sea. Stories about meteorites or other space "stuff" hitting the earth remained legend, until the Great Meteor Crater became a proving ground.

Meteor Crater is the largest crater on earth having a meteoritic origin. Proof of this origin was gained by the finding of meteorites in the surrounding area. While this crater was known as long ago as 1871, it was then thought to be a dead volcano. Shepherds found some meteorites about two miles west of the crater in 1886. This finding brought scientists to the site. In 1902 Barringer learned of the crater and bought the purportedly worthless land. His goal was to discover the meteorite which had caused the crater. Subsequent exploration and discovery of meteorites in the area led scientists to conclude that the great crater had, indeed, been created by meteoritic impact. A shower of meteorites may have hit the earth about 20,000 years ago; inevitably this date has been linked with the time Atlantis sank—or was displaced.

This same shower of meteorites is believed to have caused the Odessa group of craters in Texas. George Foster, author of *The Meteor Crater Story* (Winslow, Arizona) describes meteorites as: celestial debris that has traveled through space, probably through ages of time, until finally it strikes the earth's atmosphere. Heat generated by collision with molecules of the atmosphere vaporizes these particles, and molten material is swept off to make the fiery train we see. Usually, as most invading particles range in size from a few grains to a fraction of an ounce, vaporization is complete and the flash instantly disappears. A comparatively few stones of greater size survive that dash, at least in part, and strike the earth to supply the only material "from out of this world" that we may see and touch.

The relatively large size of the meteorites which caused the Odessa group of craters in Texas and the Great Meteor Crater in Arizona is unknown. However the dimensions of the Arizona crater give scientists a working idea of the nature and origin of the meteorite that, like legendary Atlantis, is believed still sunk in the earth.

From the crater's rim the interior depth is 570 feet. The diameter of the top around the rim is more than 4,000 feet.

The tourist walking around the rim travels for three miles before returning to his starting point.

George Foster writes, "It is now thought that this crater was made some 20,000 years ago, when a huge cluster of meteorites struck from out of the northern sky. It is believed to have weighed at least a million tons and to have been traveling at least several miles per second. It struck at an angle, drove for nearly a mile through solid rock while it was being decelerated to zero velocity, and its fragments finally came to rest below the base of the cliff directly across from here." He adds that "it is assumed that a cataclysmic explosion occurred as the impacting body was crossing what is now the center of the crater."

Twenty thousand years after the meteoritic explosion there still remain about 300 million tons of material in the crater rim. Approximately 100 million tons of sandstone were estimated to have been pulverized as fine as powdered sugar.

The meteoritic mass from interplanetary space, which made a crater large enough to dwarf the Washington Monument or Great Pyramid of Egypt, is composed of 92 percent iron, 7 percent nickel, plus between 1 and 2 percent minor elements including phosphorous, silicon, copper, and carbon, and small amounts of platinum, iridium, cobalt, gold, silver, and even microscopic diamonds. Crystals of silicon carbide, the only natural carborundum on earth, were also found in meteorites near the crater. Their presence is testimony to the tremendous heat and pressure under which these meteorites were formed.

The meteoritic mass is presumed to have been traveling between 30,000 and 33,000 miles per hour. When the earth was struck, a force of a multimegaton hydrogen bomb displaced half a billion tons of rock from the crater and possibly destroyed all plant and animal life within a 100-mile area.

While major study has been done at the Great Meteor Crater, scientists working with meteorites from the Odessa, Texas, group of craters concluded that craters in both sites were caused by the same shower of meteors. The distance between the Meteor Crater and the Odessa group is 550 miles. This is the greatest separation of known craters produced by one fall. These craters are above sea level. It is possible that the same meteorite shower that produced the craters of the American Southwest also created craters yet undiscovered, unrecognized as being from the same area, or eluding human study because they are underground, under grass, or undersea.

If a meteorite of the size and intensity of the one that struck Arizona's semidesert region, impacting with the power of a multimegaton bomb, hit the ocean waters near Atlantis, the force of impact and explosion would hypothetically turn the waters to vapor or pure gaseous energy. In other words, the ocean waters would instantly disintegrate, just as desert rock was pulverized to powderlike dust.

As nature returned to a calm balance, the elements displaced by the impact would eventually reform as moisture in the atmosphere. Torrential rains would fall; ultimately the waters would return to the sea. There would be a major difference, however. A vast crater would now exist at the sea bottom where none had been before. Waters would rush in to fill up the hole. An undertow, or sucking tide below the surface of the sea, would result as waters rushed to fill the crater. The effect would be one of suction—and any land mass displaced by this suction would experience a series of shock waves or earthquakes prior to inundation.

Astrogeology and meteorology are two new branches of science, the former being born in the past quarter century and the latter being only about a century and a half old. They may one day correlate with archaeology in the writing of man's full ancient and modern history.

To date the great meteor which gouged a mouth-like crater in the Arizona desert has not been found, despite nearly 30 years of effort by Barringer, whose diggings merely uncovered the major surface debris in the great crater's pit. Although it is not a part of the U.S. National Park Service, Meteor Crater was designated a natural landmark by the service in 1967. In 1971, the designation was changed to National Natural Landmark. The Barringer Crater Company has leased the tourist rights to the crater to Meteor Crater Enterprises, Inc., a corporation formed by the stockholders of "Bar T Bar Ranch, Inc.," whose lands surround the crater. Expiration date of this lease is the year 2157. A museum as well as a site for scientific study exists on the rim of the world's largest natural laboratory. Among those who use the facilities are such diverse groups as touring schoolchildren and National Aeronautics and Space Administration (NASA) scientists.

At the present time, two hypotheses regarding the Great Meteor are:

(1) Its crystal structure indicates many of the meteorites in the shower of 20,000 years ago might be parts of a disrupted planet which possibly once traveled on an orbit located between those of Mars and Jupiter.

(2) Most authorities believe the meteorite which formed the Great Meteor Crater struck from the north.

There is little agreement about the actual size of the great missing meteorite. E. Opik of Armagh Observatory, Ireland, calculated that the crater was caused by the fall at about 12 miles per second of a body approximately two million tons and resembling an iron sphere approximately 260 feet in diameter.

The arid Arizona desert is halfway around the world from any purported site of sunken Atlantis. The correlations between a cataclysm in the American southwest and destruction of a civilization in the Aegean Sea of Greece are indirect. There is, however, as distinct a link between the Odessa group of craters and the Great Meteor Crater as there is between the two sites of the craters and the unknown site of sunken Atlantis. That correlation is: *displacement*. Where there exists a crater, there is also evidence of solid matter, liquid, or gas that has been displaced. Craters therefore hold clues to the crucial question: where did our missing civilizations go?

Since 1790 only 22 authenticated cases of meteorites striking and/or damaging buildings have been recorded. Dr. Lincoln LaPaz of the Department of Mathematics and Astronomy and the Institute of Meteoritics, University of New Mexico, calculated in 1951 that perhaps one person out of three would be struck by a meteorite during this century. A few days after he made his statement at a meeting sponsored jointly by the USAF School of Aviation Medicine and the Lovelace Foundation for Medical Education and Research, at San Antonio, Texas, a stony meteorite penetrated the roof of a Sylacauga, Alabama, home. Mrs. E. Hulitt Hodges was stricken while lying down, covered by two quilts. The stone which richocheted off the walls, bruising her hip, weighed nine pounds.

A smaller fragment of the meteoritic stone that hit Mrs. Hodges fell several miles distant on the farm of J. K. McKinney. Again, separation of meteorites in one fall occurred—on a small scale.

There is no evidence known that refutes the theory that a larger meteorite, or shower of meteorites, could have fallen to earth, resulting in the extinction of a large population, and the ground on which it lived. The Arizona and Odessa craters are testimony that something fell with great impact from somewhere. If other meteorites fell from the same shower on different parts of the earth, Atlantis may have been a prime target. Somewhere beneath the sea's surface there may exist not only a sunken civilization but one or more craters that displaced a culture which became a legend in the ripples of the seas of man's imagination.

The Great Meteor Crater of Arizona is the first proven meteoritic crater. It offers mankind an opportunity to further study and correlate the displacement effects such a natural catastrophe can have on the entire surface of the earth, and its residents. The impact that created Great Meteor Crater is estimated to have killed all flora and fauna within a 100-mile radius. Would such a meteor have had a similar effect on plant and animal life if it struck the ocean with equivalent force?

The surface of our planet is 70 percent water. Perhaps the answers to the crater effect theory lie below the sea's surface. If the crater effect theory is valid as regards the disappearance of Atlantis, either a volcanic crater or a meteoritic crater, probably located under the seas, holds the clue for understanding how and why Atlantis disappeared. On a surface level, the effects of a volcano eruption from the bowels of the earth, and a meteorite streaking like fire into the atmosphere, then exploding, would be similar: the land would shake, the waters boil, torrential rains would fall. Next target, therefore: a search for undersea craters.

CHAPTER 10

From Atlantis to Hawaii

Hawaiians have long believed that when God, or the gods, take away part of the earth's surface, a replacement in like amount of substance or form is made elsewhere on the planet's surface. A modern day Kahuna descendent of the islands' priestly caste, who calls himself simply Doctor Karl, explains the theory this way:

"Just as modern science knows that water displaces its own weight, so does matter displace its own weight. If you have a bathtub filled with water and you take a bucket and bail out half the water from one end of the tub, you don't have a large hole where the water disappeared. Instead, the remaining water rushes in to fill up the hole created by removal of the water.

"When we Hawaiians who follow the old religion speak of the spirits, we often refer to natural laws such as the water law. There is Divine Intelligence in all that is Created. This is true of water, rocks, wind or living beings in flesh or non-incarnate. The spirits we speak of can be better understood if it is known that 'spirit' refers to that innate intelligence, the 'something' that causes the water to displace its own weight."

By profession, Doctor Karl is a tour bus driver on the island of Hawaii, known as "the big island." He took the name Karl shortly after the Hawaiian territory became a U.S. state. "Karl is a *haole* [foreign] name," he says. "Mainlanders, largely white people, can identify more easily with a name like Karl than a long Hawaiian name in many syllables. The wise man or woman knows that it is easier to live among people when you speak their own language. English is the main language in the Hawaiian Islands, so I took an English name—on the surface.

"The reason for so much conflict between science and religion and politics and other surface expressions of truth lies in the fact that people are all speaking different languages. We Hawaiians attribute volcanic eruption, for example, to the goddess Pele, or Madame Pele. Your western scientists have other explanations, more scientific ones.

"The fact remains, however, that a volcanic eruption is still a volcanic eruption, whatever the human explanation. When a volcano explodes, something is moved. If something is moved, as in the case of lava, then that displaced matter is replaced—by air, water or other matter moving somewhere.

"The elements that move may be physical, liquid or gaseous in nature, but the non-identifiable prime mover is spiritual—or intelligent—in nature."

Doctor Karl is an eschatologist. "I study the book of life and try to help others understand it," he says. Tour bus driving gives him an income; his more spiritual work is done for no charge. "When the white men came to the Hawaiian islands and converted our people to Christianity, our old religion did not die. It merely went underground.

"In the days before telephones, radios or televisions were invented, we used a simple form of communication from island to island. Today it is known as ESP. We sent and received thoughts, sometimes hundreds of miles. How else could we have communicated from island to island? The telepathic ability to communicate is a natural one. The person who can communicate with his fellow man through this method can also communicate with the 'spirits' of intelligent beings non-incarnate. Thus, the Hawaiian people were, and many still are, very attuned to nature.

"Through this ability to attune with nature, man is able to predict forthcoming cataclysms. It is really very simple. Man receives the vibrations long before an actual manifestation occurs to cause a volcanic disturbance or tidal wave. If man is prepared, he can take measures to avoid being harmed. I know of no one during my lifetime who has been harmed or killed by volcanic eruptions, even though the Big Island is the largest new piece of land being born today on the face of the earth."

Doctor Karl says that the Hawaiian people might have come originally from the sunken continent of Atlantis or its Pacific Ocean legendary counterpart, Lemuria or Mu.

"Our origin is not documented. There is evidence that the Hawaiian people are offspring of the more southerly Polynesian peoples. Hawaiian legend says that small groups of survivors of a cataclysm that occurred thousands of years ago drifted in boats in the seas. There is a story that says that a coconut once fell into the sea and drifted north, and a large wave washed it onto an island. The coconut became rooted and grew into a tree. It dropped its fruit into the seas and more coconuts were washed ashore. Eventually coconuts were growing on the islands nearby, and when the first Hawaiian people arrived by boat there was food for them to eat. Like the coconuts, these first people planted their roots on the islands. Many of them stayed, while other groups drifted farther north and populated the islands now known as the Philippines and Guam, and even Japan."

The Hawaiian racial theory differs from scientific theory of the population of the Americas. The latter idea holds that groups of people crossed the Bering Straits and moved south, crossing the land now known as Alaska, Canada, and North America, and eventually moving south into Central and South America. Many of the art objects and physical features of South American Indians resemble those of the early Hawaiian people.

According to the theory proposed by Doctor Karl, a cataclysm occurred in the Southern Hemisphere, which displaced portions of a now-extinct civilization. These survivors traveled north by boat, eventually moving as far as Japan. Others may have traveled in easterly or westerly directions, settling on some of the more southerly islands, such as Samoa or the Easter Islands, making their habitat the regions of South or Central America.

"I do not speak for all the Hawaiian people," Doctor Karl says. "But I do speak the feelings and beliefs of those who maintain contact with the old religion."

He says that while the Hawaiians may have appeared to the first Christian settlers and missionaries as uncivilized and pagan, "we actually possessed keen enough knowledge to realize that one day we Hawaiians may displace white man."

This knowledge is not merely intuitive, unsubstantial speculation. It is based on understanding the principle of displacement—which might have caused the displacement of Atlantean or Lemurian inhabitants, resulting in the intermingling of these people with inhabitants of many Pacific islands, such intermingling causing the differences in physical characteristics among different island groups. As Doctor Karl says, "As the Big Island is being born through volcanic eruption, something somewhere is being displaced. We believe evidence of this displacement can be found along the shorelines of the Continental United States. Portions of the coastline are slowly sinking. As this is happening, sporadic lava spills are slowly building up the Big Island."

Doctor Karl predicts that "if the day comes when the Big Island erupts in cataclysmic explosion—similar to that which may have destroyed Atlantis—parts of the United States will sink. The West Coast, particularly California where measurable sinking of the coastal shores is known to occur, is the prime candidate for this replacement. The sinking could occur in one of two ways; either through tidal waves caused by hot molten matter being dumped into the Pacific Ocean and causing surface disturbance; or, through undersea suction as waters rush to fill in the hole caused under the surface of the ocean floor when hot molten matter is spat up through the volcanic opening. Then, water would rush in to fill the hole. This would create an under-surface suction, the effect of which could draw portions of the coastline into the sea. When the waters settled, there would be a new coastline.

"We Hawaiians who are aware of the workings of nature through displacement also realize that our services may be needed by survivors of such a catastrophe. Perhaps the time will come when we must sail to white man in our boats, as Captain Cook once sailed to our islands, and deliver a message of truth. This, of course, depends on what happens here."

"Here" refers to the island of Hawaii, which can be traveled by car in less than one day's driving time. A traveler visiting the island can drive around the coastal areas on enough gasoline to cover about 300 total miles. But this small piece of solid land in the Pacific Ocean is growing.

Tourism, too, is exanding, as mainlanders overcome their fears of volcanic eruptions and flock to this small island annually. Many Americans, hitherto afraid of owning land on the island of Hawaii, have virtually bought all the available sites. Not all the land on the Big Island is habitable, however. Two active volcanoes prevent settlers from laying stake to grounds higher up on the island.

In 1916 Congress created a national park in the island of

Hawaii. This national park, under the American flag, consisted of a beautiful, placid place of coral reefs, tropical palms, abundant flowers, pineapples, earthquakes, and volcanoes.

Mauna Loa, which rises 13,680 feet, is sometimes called "the greatest of all living volcanoes." Around its peak hangs a vaporous cloud, a billowing gray testimony to the fact that man's technology has not been able to bring sunshine to this mountaintop, nor to suppress the natural forces of Creation.

Kilauea volcano, known for its "lake of fire," is around 4,000 feet in height. Unlike Mauna Loa, which erupts, Kilauea volcano is likened to a boiling pot of lava. Hawaiians call the volcano *Halemaumau*, meaning "the house of everlasting fire."

Tour buses arrive at the rim of Kilauea volcano daily. Venturesome tourists can peer into openings in the earth and be treated to gusty bursts of hot steam, saunas for the face and neck.

The visitor to this site experiences a strange feeling akin to that which the astronauts must have felt when they stepped upon the moon's surface. The terrain is surprisingly flat, extending for hundreds of yards. The lack of lush foliage, so evident on the slopes of the island, creates the illusion of being in dead but virgin territory. Everything is a brownish-gray color.

The appearance of the volcano's surface is similar to the surface of the Great Meteor Crater in Arizona—a vast round hole sunk into the earth, with its flatness extending beneath circular walls that rise up to meet the sky.

Walkways are continually being established in "safe" zones. The unpredictable appearance of new cinder cones beneath and around the crater are proof that this placid, quiet volcanic zone is not as safe as it appears on the surface. The surface today may be replaced tomorrow. Visitors remark that they feel they know what the earth's surface would look like after a nuclear holocaust, when viewing the volcano. Most visitors are happy to leave this place.

Not even the most telepathically astute native Hawaiian can offer an explanation. "We live philosophically," says Doctor Karl. "Hilo, our main city on the Big Island, was practically wiped out by a tidal wave. We moved up the slopes when the waters hit. When the volcano erupts, spitting fire into the sky, we gauge the direction in which the lava will flow and we move down the slopes to avoid it.

"If someday the island blows, instead of grows, some of us will get out by plane. Others may get out by boat. The rest? We'll probably sink, as legend says happened thousands of years ago in Atlantis. This time, however, if one civilization is displaced by another, there's enough scientific evidence around to prove to man that lost civilizations that sank aren't just stories.

"Maybe it will take a great tragedy to make man realize that nature displaces nations, and even the men who live in them. Your *haole* prophet, Edgar Cayce, said that when earthquakes hit Japan and volcanic eruptions hit Hawaii, the coastline of California might go. He also spoke of life in ancient Atlantis. The question is not so much 'when will it happen' as 'are you prepared if it does happen?' When nature explodes, man has little choice but to go along with the phenomena, surviving as best he can.

"Wherever you find a crater, you find evidence that natural displacement has occurred somewhere else. Perhaps Atlantis sank when the Hawaiian Islands were being born. Water is the great medium which balances the earth's surface changes. The distance in miles has no bearing on the action of this natural law. If a whole continent such as Atlantis did sink, something somewhere had to rise. The earth is one small unified planet, one body in space. Distance, as man measures it, is infinitesimal compared to the vastness of all space. If the Island of Hawaii were to explode and tons of lava spilled out from the earth's inner parts, and California were to sink, it would be a minute physical change—a balancing—in infinity.

"For every mountain there is a potential sunken island or continent. Understanding this principle of displacement makes it easier to accept the belief that, yes, Atlantis was a very real place, and yes, the Hawaiian people of today might have at one time been survivors of that civilization. It is not improbable. It seems feasible. We came from somewhere. The question is, where?"

CHAPTER 11

Volcanic Parallels

What did hit Atlantis? The list of hypothetical calamities could go on endlessly, but the most commonly occurring natural disaster on this planet—with effects like those described by Plato—is volcanic eruption.

Volcanism is an integral part of the geological process that forms the earth's crust, the rising and falling of mountain ranges and the tearing open of great rifts. In fact, because of the constantly changing nature of the earth's surface, there is probably no part of the world that has not at some time in the past been the scene of volcanic activity. As evidence of this, most of the five hundred and some volcanoes that are active today lie in a belt that encircles the Pacific Ocean and coincides generally with regions of recent mountain-building. There are also pockets of volcanoes in Iceland, the Azores, the Mediterranean, and southeast Africa.

There are many kinds of volcanoes. Some are enormous mountains, thousands of feet high, capped with snow; some are mere fissures in rock formations; others (probably many more than we know) are hidden under the sea. Volcanoes most often are classified by type of eruption, both as to strength of explosion and volume of material ejected. One distinctive type, the Hawaiian, is characterized by fountains of lava that spurt from the top or side of the volcano and flow down into the surrounding areas. Another type, the Strombolian, rhythmically ejects incandescent cinder, while the Peléean features the formation of domes and glowing avalanches of matter and gas. There are other variations.

Regardless of type, volcanoes have always inspired and terrified mankind. Their destructive capacity is awesome: A lava flow, though it advances very slowly, engulfs and incinerates everything in its path. It it flows onto snow or ice, it generates floods of mud flows that also engulf fields and towns. A heavy ash fall destroys all vegetation within a radius of many miles of the volcano. It destroys grazing animals as well, partly by starvation and partly by clogging their digestive systems. It also can cause respiratory irritation in people and animals and, indirectly, a wide range of other disorders. A glowing avalanche, like a lava flow, wipes out everything in its path. Volcanic gases can kill or adversely affect people, animals, and vegetation. A volcanic eruption, particularly if accompanied by an earthquake or tidal wave—as is often the case—can utterly decimate miles of countryside, and the sights and sounds of the spectacle stagger the imagination.

If we assume that Professor Marinatos and others are correct in the theory that Atlantis was Crete, destroyed in 1500 B.C. by the eruption of Thera, we can, to some degree, reconstruct what happened. The prehistoric crater found in the ocean and encompassing what is now Santorini is 32 square miles in area. Its size elevates the crater to the classification of caldera, a formation which is associated with a Plinian type of eruption.

A typical Plinian eruption can be described as follows: Volcanic activity begins with mild explosions of pumice and ash from the cone (summit) of the volcano. The pumice and ash are thrown high in the air and blanket the surrounding area. At this point, the magma (volcanic matter), which has been standing high in the conduit leading to the cone of the volcano, begins to recede. The explosions increase in violence, and the magma recedes farther down the conduit into the main volcanic chamber underground. The culminating explosions fling even more pumice and ash into the air, and glowing avalanches and/or ash flows can occur and be more voluminous than the air-fall debris, though it is not always the case. By now the magma level is deep in the chamber. The walls of the cone, weakened by the explosions and lacking the support of the magma, crumble and collapse into the chamber. The volcano now looks as though it has been decapitated. In place of the cone and former crater is an enormous caldera. In time, new cones can develop on the floor of the caldera.

This type of volcano is named after Pliny the Elder, the famous Roman naturalist who died in the eruption of Vesuvius in A.D. 79, but it was Pliny the Younger, his nephew, who recorded the event for posterity. From the account of the

Younger Pliny, in the form of letters to the historian, Tacitus, combined with later geological studies, we are able to deduce what happened when Vesuvius erupted.

It began in A.D. 63 with the first of a series of earthquakes that, over the next few years, did great damage to the cities near the foot of the mountain. The Romans, however, failed to recognize the beginning of an eruptive cycle (the volcano had been dormant probably thousands of years) and were surprised when a cloud appeared over the mountain on August 24, A.D. 79. Light-colored ash and pumice began to fall. The Elder Pliny, who was then an admiral in command of a fleet, took his galleys across the Bay of Naples toward the mountain where he could better observe the eruption and also be available to rescue any friends in need. The shore had been heaved up several feet so that he was unable to land, so he took his ships southward to Stabiae, where he intended to spend the night. In the course of the night he and his companions decided it best to flee, and, tying pillows to their heads to protect them from falling rocks, they took to the fields. During the flight, Pliny, who was very fat, died apparently of a heart attack. In the meantime, the Younger Pliny, who was in the vicinity of Mycenae, was experiencing the same heavy fall of ash and pumice, with impenetrable darkness, earthquakes, and terrifying fluctuations in the shoreline.

In the end, the ejections of ash and pumice from Vesuvius buried Pompeii and Stabiae. As the magma receded and new explosions occurred, the cone of the mountain fell in on iteself three times, and lava escaped from a vent on the north. A heavy rain began and saturated the ash and pumice deposits on the west, creating the mud flows that buried Herculaneum. At last, weak from the explosions and lacking support, the upper mountain collapsed a final time, so that all that was left of the former 6,000-foot edifice was an enormous caldera. Vesuvius lay dormant then for nearly a century, but new, smaller eruptions have since built another cone. The present Mount Vesuvius stands in the remains of the old one, known as Monte Somma.

Closer to home and even more spectacular was the eruption of what is now called Mount Mazama, in the Cascade Mountain Range of Oregon. Like other volcanoes in the region, Mazama was active during and following the Ice Age.

From the size of the depressions left by glaciers on the lip of the present caldera, geologists estimate the original height of the mountain to have been about twelve thousand feet.

The first explosions of the caldera-forming eruption, heard only by prehistoric Indians, undoubtedly were of the usual Plinian type. There must have been an earthquake and then, above the summit, the appearance of white vapor. Within a few hours, as the content of the ash increased, the vapor would have changed into an ominous black column, and as days went by, the rumbling of the mountain would have grown louder and the size of the falling fragments increased. Showers of fine ash fell hundreds of miles away, east and northeast of the volcano. When the preliminary eruptions ended, geologists have confirmed, there was a mantle of ash covering thousands of square miles. On the mountain itself, pumice was more than 50 feet deep, and 70 miles away it was six inches deep. Then probably followed a period of disarming quiet. But another puff of vapor would have signaled the final catastrophic explosions. The puff would have grown into an immense cloud. Then an ear-splitting roar, and the cloud would have branched and hurtled down the sides of the mountain at speeds up to a hundred miles an hour. Beneath the cloud, hidden from distant view, was an avalanche of glowing ash and pumice that scorched the earth in a 35-mile radius. The ground shook; there was a tumultuous roar; then quiet. In a few days, the winds would have cleared the clouds away and revealed what was left of the once snow-capped mountain: a caldera five to six miles wide and 4,000 feet deep. Seventeen cubic miles of the mountaintop had disappeared into the chamber below.

We cannot know how long the volcano lay dormant after that, but centuries later a small cinder cone formed in the caldera. From the age of the oldest trees on the cone, it would appear that the last eruptions in the caldera occurred no more than a thousand years ago. A lake formed. The caldera is now known as Crater Lake, and the cone as Wizard Island. The area, one of the scenic wonders of the United States, is a national park visited annually by thousands of people.

The preceding two cases are perfect examples of caldera-forming eruptions. However, the eruption on the Indonesian island of Krakatoa in 1883 most nearly parallels the one that destroyed Thera and, possibly, Crete. The Krakatoa eruption certainly was one of the world's most dramatic and best documented.

Krakatoa, like Thera, is an island volcano. Before the eruption of 1883, the visible part of the volcano consisted of three small islands: Krakatoa, Verlaten, and Lang. These were projections along the rim of a prehistoric caldera on the ocean floor. The largest, Krakatoa Island, consisted of three overlapping cones: the oldest and largest was Rakata; Danan and Perbuwatan were successively younger and smaller. The last activity had been from Perbuwatan 200 years before.

On May 20, the volcano returned to activity, again with moderate explosions from Perbuwatan. People in the area took the event so lightly that a week later, when the eruptions had subsided somewhat, a steamer was chartered to visit Krakatoa Island (which was uninhabited). The visitors found a column of steam blasting from an opening about thirty yards wide and a fine layer of ash which had killed all vegetation on the island.

There was no more activity until June 19, when the explosions resumed. A few days later a second vent opened on Danan. On August 11, the last time the island was visited before the final eruptions, a group of observers reported three main vents, all mildly active. No one was alarmed. As late as August 25, a local newspaper noted: "Fine weather, no extraordinary detonations in the afternoon."

On August 26, at 1 P.M., the first of a series of tremendous explosions occurred, and a cloud of black ash rose above Krakatoa to a height of 17 miles. Observers on a ship in the area, the *Charles Bal*, reported that the clouds driven to the east had the appearance of a furious squall. At 5 P.M. the first caldera collapse occurred, and the seismic shock created a *tsunami* that swamped harbors and shorelines of nearby Java and Sumatra. Ships in the area reported disturbances in the sea, but did not realize what was happening. Inhabitants in the area, who had for weeks been accustomed to noise from Krakatoa, still were not unduly disturbed.

Things got worse during the night. The noise was incessant. No one in western Java was able to sleep, and the explosions were heard in Batavia 100 miles away. There were severe air shocks, though no earthquakes. The crew of the *Charles Bal*, anchored 11 miles southeast of Krakatoa, had an anxious night. According to the ship's log, " ... chains of fire appeared to descend and ascend between the sky and the island, while on the south-west end there seemed to be a continued roll of balls of white fire; the wind, though strong, was hot and choking, sulphurous, with a smell as of burning cinders, some of the pieces falling on us being like iron cinders, and the lead from a bottom of 30 fathoms came up quite warm. From midnight to 4 A.M. (27th) wind strong, but very unsteady between south-south-west and west-south-west, impenetrable darkness continuing, the roaring of Krakatoa less continuous, but more explosive in sound, the sky one second intense blackness, and the next a blaze of fire; masthead and yardarms studded with corposants, and a peculiarly pinkish flame coming from the clouds, which seemed to touch the mastheads and yardarms."

Between 4 and 7 A.M. the morning of August 27, several *tsunamis* spread outward from Krakatoa, probably due to additional caldera collapses. But the worst was yet to come. At 10 A.M. there was a detonation that was heard 3,000 miles away by the coast guard on Rodriguez Island. A half an hour later there was a 120-foot tidal wave that swept the shores of Java and Sumatra, destroying 295 towns and killing 36,000 people. The rain of mud and ash from this most violent of explosions continued for hours. Some ships were carried miles inland: others were unable to navigate in the sea of floating pumice.

A survivor of the *tsunami* said: " ... I heard a cry, 'The flood comes.' On looking around I saw a high wave which I could not escape; I was lifted from the ground, but caught hold of a tree. Then I perceived several waves, which followed the first; the place where Anjer had been before was covered by a turbulent sea, from which some trees and roofs of houses were still peeping out. After the wave had flowed off, I left the tree, and found myself in the midst of the devastation."

The ash cloud resulting from the explosion rose 50 miles in the air and darkened areas as far as 275 miles away. Dust spread out in the upper atmosphere and was carried around the earth several times by air currents. Sun rays reaching the earth's surface the following year were estimated to be about 87 percent normal, and the resulting glows before sunrise and after sunset attracted worldwide attention for months. (On

October 30, 1883, alarmed citizens called out fire engines in Poughkeepsie, N.Y., and New Haven, Conn.!)

There were a few milder, intermittent explosions and waves, but by midmorning of August 28 the eruption was essentially over. Two-thirds of Krakatoa was missing: Perbuwatan and Danan were completely gone, and Rakata was chopped in half. What was left was a two-basin caldera, approximately nine hundred feet below sea level and five miles in diameter. Above sea level were the stump of Rakata and two small new islands, projections of the rim of the new caldera.

Krakatoa remained quiet less than half a century. In 1927 fishermen discovered gas bubbles and, at night, a red glow in the area halfway between the former location of Danan and Perbuwatan. The next year an island appeared, disappeared, reappeared several times. A few explosions took place, but the new vent remained essentially underwater until 1952. At that time a 200-foot cinder cone emerged, which, by 1959 had been extended by yet a newer cone within its crater. The island continues to grow. It is called Anak Krakatoa—"Child of Krakatoa."

Professor Marinatos, James Mavor, and Anton Galanapoulos have favorably compared the eruptions of Krakatoa and Thera. The caldera at Thera is almost five times the size of Krakatoa and the ash residue in the area is supposedly thicker and wider spread. This would suggest a more violent explosion than Krakatoa, though the evidence is inconclusive. It is known that Krakatoa emitted greater power than many larger cones. But if the magnitude of the explosion at Thera was, indeed, as great as or greater than that of Krakatoa, and if the resulting *tsunamis* were comparable, then the effect of the eruption upon nearby Crete, in fact upon the entire Mediterranean area, would have been devastating.

CHAPTER 12

"We Believe This Was Atlantis!"

Plato's description of the location of Atlantis " . . . west of the straits which you call the Pillars of Hercules . . ." has been interpreted by some seekers to mean west of the Straits of Gibraltar, off the coasts of Spain and northern Africa. One of the most energetic proponents of this theory is Maxine Asher, a California educator and psychic researcher, who is founder and director of an organization called the Ancient Mediterranean Research Association (AMRA). In 1973 Dr. Asher led an expedition to Spain and attempted to combine the skills of physical scientists and psychics to find the lost continent. Her expedition aroused an unprecedented amount of public interest at its inception and an equal amount of criticism of its outcome.

Mrs. Asher was a public school teacher when, in 1960, she decided to go back to college to take a summer course in ancient history. She became so enamored of the subject that she decided to pursue an M.A. degree in ancient and medieval history. Being an energetic woman, she had no trouble doing this while continuing to supervise her three children and to write at home. When she got her degree she went on to teach history at a small California college, all the while keeping up her interest in the field of education as well. Challenges did present themselves. From her point of view, societal biases against her as a woman (a blond woman at that), a psychic researcher, and a revolutionary educator were the cause of her scrapes with academic officialdom.

Eventually her interest in antiquity narrowed to civilizations predating known empires, and she began a series of field trips in search of buried cities. Her research, which had been somewhat diffuse, came into focus when she came across the book *Atlantis: The Truth Behind the Legend*, by Anghelos Galanopoulous; Maxine Asher was startled by the realization

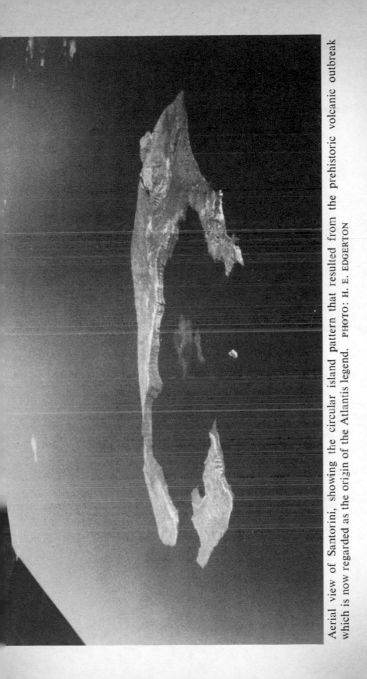

Aerial view of Santorini, showing the circular island pattern that resulted from the prehistoric volcanic outbreak which is now regarded as the origin of the Atlantis legend.   PHOTO: H. E. EDGERTON

Here's a drawing of Thera today. Taken from the book *Voyage to Atlantis*, by James W. Mavor, Jr. (Putnam, 1969).

Jacques Cousteau, discussing his underwater exploration of the Aegean Sea with Tzannis Tzannetakis, Secretary General of the Greek National Tourist Organization.

The *S.S. Calypso*, Jacques Cousteau's exploration vessel, anchored in the port of Passelemani (Piraeus), Greece.

Ignatius Donnelly, whose research and writings on Atlantis created a pattern of ideas that has influenced the work of others for the past century. MINNESOTA HISTORICAL SOCIETY

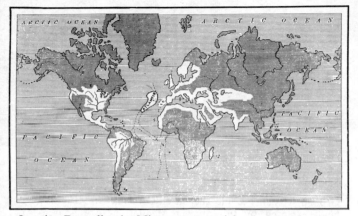

Ignatius Donnelly, the Minnesota maverick whose work *Atlantis: The Antediluvian World* (1882) had a profound and lasting effect on popular views on this subject, envisioned that Atlanteans migrated to, colonized, and culturally influenced the extensive areas that stand out in white on this map; these include much of the coastal areas of Europe, the Mediterranean, North Africa, and substantial sections of North and South America.

Dr. Maxine Asher, with her associate, Paco Salazar, examining an urn brought to the surface of the ocean off Cadiz, Spain.

Ground segments of the ancient city of Dun An Aenghus, Ireland, explored by the Ancient Mediterranean Research Association and considered by it as possibly a part of Atlantis.

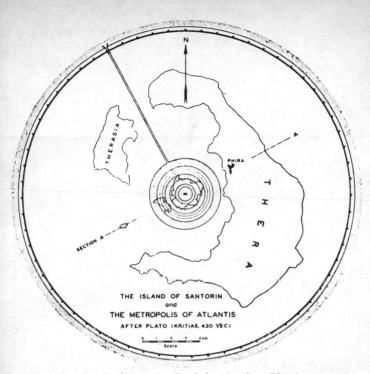

THE ISLAND OF SANTORIN
and
THE METROPOLIS OF ATLANTIS
AFTER PLATO (KRITIAS, 430 VBC)

As viewed by Professor A. G. Galanopoulos, Plato's account of Atlantis in his *Critias* suggests that the Atlantean metropolis was located in the very center of today's Santorini-Thera crater, where the two Kamenis islets reemerged in the late nineteenth century In the above drawing, Galanopoulos has superimposed Plato's Atlantis on Thera. Within the concentric rings in the center, temples to Poseidon and Cleito would have been situated, with residential areas, waterways, guard houses, altars, and even a race course completing the city. A palace, possibly along lines similar to the one unearthed in Knossos (Crete), would have been situated in the central temple area.

This drawing, cautiously called a "Conjectural Map of Atlantis" and published in 1803 by the French cartographer Bory de Saint-Vincent, is based on the assumption that various island groups within the Atlantic Ocean, including the Azores and the Canaries, were remnants of the Lost Continent.

that what she had been looking for all along was Atlantis. Intuitively, though, she rejected Galanopoulous' claim that he had found Atlantis on Crete. She felt that he may have found an Atlantean colony, but not Atlantis, and she proceeded to launch her own search.

She read Atlantean literature and traveled extensively, interviewing and photographing in Spain, the Canary Islands, Ireland, and the Greek Islands. In the meantime, she tried to get into several American doctoral programs, but was turned down because of the language requirements. Undaunted, she enrolled in the Spanish university system and used her spare time to continue to search for clues to Atlantis.

It seemed no coincidence to her that the same patterns of concentric spirals appeared in petroglyphs of the guanches on the Canary Islands, in the caves of New Grange, Ireland, and in many Mediterranean areas. She felt that these spirals might represent the Atlantean capital city, which Plato had described as circular. On intuition, she photographed some scratches on the rock leading up to Gibraltar. The scratches were later identified by a linguist, Dr. Cyrus Gordon of New York University, as a language, as yet untranslatable. In addition, she found other unexplained inscriptions in volcanic rock in caves in southern Spain which bore remarkable resemblances to inscriptions in the Pyrenees and in Ireland. Because of these and other clues, but more because of a strong hunch (Mrs. Asher does not discount the possibility that she is a reincarnated Atlantean), she decided that the best place to look for Atlantis was in the waters off southwestern Spain, near Cádiz.

By the summer of 1973, Mrs. Asher had founded the AMRA and recruited her old history teacher, Dr. Julian Nava, president of the Los Angeles Board of Education, to serve as codirector of an expedition to Spain. She planned to enlist students, teachers, researchers, and experts in various fields, as well as psychics, to help in the search. Unable to finance the project alone (her husband was a stockbroker), she suggested that Pepperdine College, a small liberal arts school in Los Angeles, adopt it as a six-credit summer course. A school spokesman, however, made clear to the press at the time that Pepperdine did not necessarily support any theories about Atlantis, but endorsed the investigative methods Mrs. Asher and her group would employ.

Plans for the expedition were impressive. Mrs. Asher thought she would take along about two hundred students (at $1,995 each) and an unspecified number of other interested people (at nearly $3,000 each). Other backing would come from donations and from AMRA members. In an interview with Walt Murray for the August 1973 issue of *Probe* magazine, she provided a long list of expedition personnel: Egerton Sykes, dean of Atlantean lore, would be a consultant. Brendan Doyle, chief photographer for the Irish Museum, would teach photography classes. Bruce Rosendahl of the Scripps Institute would direct diving. Mary Smith of the Archives of the Indies in Seville, Spain, would attempt to collect and process data left by Christopher Columbus and other European sources. Dr. John Hartley, professor of Linguistics at Azusa College, would bring along a massive collection of Phoenician inscriptions on photo slides. Dr. J. Manson Valentine, who had recently explored Atlantean possibilities off Bimini, and Gail Cayce, granddaughter of the famed late psychic, would bring with them the voluminous files of Edgar Cayce's Atlantis readings. Michael Hughes and Jim Hart would serve as expedition psychics. And there would be numerous other American and European psychologists, geologists, archaeologists, and oceanographers. Drs. Nava and Asher, of course, would be codirectors, but overseeing all these people and their talents would be Bill Schell, director of audiovisual service for the La Mesa Schools, and Dr. Rhoda Freeman, Los Angeles city school principal.

Though she was careful to select well-trained people for the expedition, Mrs. Asher insisted that credentials were not first priority. More important, she said, were "heart, soul, and caring, and wanting to do something for the world." Furthermore, "negative vibrations" were strictly prohibited—they all were to think positively. And there would be no pulling of rank. Amateurs and experts would work together because: "Regardless of academic degrees, we're all novices in the problems of Atlantis."

In addition to the staff and their sundry specialized equipment, the group would travel with an entire library on Atlantis, as well as audiovisual equipment and photographic gear. They would arrive, via Iberia Airlines ("Is there an Atlantis? Iberia says yes."), in Seville, then transfer to the deluxe Isecotal Hotel in Cádiz, where they would set up a daily routine. There would be "flexible modular scheduling with everyone individually programmed ... In the morning, the students had small group discussions, lab sessions, lectures by experts such as Sykes. In the afternoon, [there would be] archaeological scuba diving, jewelry making from Atlantean models, Spanish lessons." The plan was to stay for six weeks, and, Dr. Asher was quite confident, they would find remnants of Atlantis—or at the very least a buried city. She based her ideas on previous undersea research she had conducted with a Spanish diver, Francisco Salazar Casero.

Dr. Asher made it plain that she obtained some of her Atlantean evidence through ESP and that she was relying on certain psychic vibrations drawn from the area to help the expedition. It was this emphasis on intuitive knowledge, combined with a systematic scientific method, that drew criticism from many American academicians. Dr. Asher, however, veteran of this kind of criticism, responded by pointing to the intuitive discoveries of such nineteenth-century archaeological heroes as Heinrich Schliemann, who discovered Troy and Mycenae, and Marcel Marcelino, who dated the 20,000-year-old cave drawings at Altamira long before the physical means to do so ever existed. The so-called scientific approach to discovering the past, she said, had been overemphasized by twentieth-century archaeologists.

The number of students who actually went on the trip—about forty-five—was far fewer than had been anticipated. There were roughly an equal number of nonmatriculated lay people. Most, but not all, of the original roster of professional people went along. Such researchers as geographer Robert Seger and anthropologist Joseph Tomchak dropped out. Dr. Nava himself, because of personal business in the United States, left the group after the first sessions but publicly supported the project throughout its difficult period in Spain.

It has never been exactly clear to the public what happened when the group reached Spain. Agreements worked out beforehand between Maxine Asher and officials of the Spanish government, which always has been reluctant to allow foreign excavators on its soil, remained in force, even though the group experienced what Dr. Asher termed "extreme harassment by unknown forces."

According to Dr. Asher, soon after the expedition reached

Cádiz, individuals in the Spanish and U.S. governments began to interfere with movements of group members. Restrictions grew daily more stringent, until finally the students were not allowed even to swim at the beach in front of the Isecotal. At that point, in an act of desperation, Asher, still in possession of the official Spanish diving permits, sent divers out in the middle of the night to a spot 12 to 14 miles off Cádiz, where she, Paco Salazar, and Egerton Sykes believed Atlantis was. The divers returned the next day with a few rolls of film and descriptions of an undersea city. Drawings were made from their descriptions (apparently, although it was developed at the hotel before witnesses, nothing conclusive was ever learned from the film), and Dr. Asher promptly issued press releases in Gibraltar and Portugal (because telephone communications in Spain were very bad) stating that they had found what they believed to be Atlantis and that it might prove to be the "greatest discovery in the history of the world."

There were storms at sea for the next two days, so the divers could not take pictures when they returned to the site. There also were storms of protest from the Spanish government, which insisted upon an immediate cessation of exploration and an inquiry into the expedition's findings. Mrs. Asher, Dr. Sykes, and three of the divers were subpoenaed to appear in the Spanish naval court.

In the meantime, other people were reacting to the press release. Olga Villespin, an archaeologist attached to the expedition by the Spanish Department of Fine Arts, told reporters: "I don't think they could have found much. They may have found early constructions but their drawings of their finding are not convincing." Ms. Villespin, however, rushed to the site after the AMRA group had left Spain, persuading Paco Salazar to show her the undersea city. Concepción Blanco, an archaeologist and curator of the archaeological museum in Cádiz, stated: "The group has issued drawings of fragments of amphorae and columns, but these look to be of the Punic era of around the third century B.C., and we've seen plenty of that around here." Cesar Peman, another archaeologist in Cádiz, said: "It's hard to take this claim seriously . . . They may have found some interesting Roman remains, but that is not so surprising near an old port like Cádiz." American newspapers picked up the story, and parents of the students involved and officials at Pepperdine grew anxious. Students themselves, unable to dive or move about at will, became discontented. Subsequently, the off-shore waters were officially closed and Spain continues to bar divers at the time of this writing.

Mrs. Asher, Dr. Sykes, and the divers appeared before the Spanish naval court and were given 10 days to get an attorney. Dr. Asher then called a meeting of the expedition and announced that the group was splitting up. Drs. Freeman, Hartley, and Gail Cayce would remain and carry on the program in Spain, while she and those who could follow would go to Ireland and try to set up the program there. Mrs. Asher was in the midst of packing and transferring power of attorney for herself to Freeman, via her lawyer, when she received word that the Spanish government was about to issue another subpoena. With no further preparation, she left Spain immediately by car, accompanied by only two members of the group. The three of them proceeded north by taxi, train, and plane in a tragicomic series of mishaps and missed connections. En route, they discovered that the power of attorney left in Cádiz was illegal, so while one of the party was sent ahead to Ireland to confirm reservations, another was sent back to Cádiz with a new, legitimate power of attorney. Dr. Asher herself eventually reached Dublin and went on to Galway where she immediately began to collect a few Irish students.

Back in Cádiz, Spanish officials apparently decided not to press charges, though they did confiscate all of the expedition's equipment and library. The group began to disperse. Some went home, but most migrated to Ireland, where they continued diving and studying the Irish connection to Atlantis. Ultimately, Pepperdine College granted them six units of credit for their work.

By that time the American press was publishing scathing accounts of the episode; European press coverage was more detached. *Newsweek* magazine ran an article—particularly damaging to Mrs. Asher's reputation and to the credibility of the find—in which John Sims, official spokesman for the AMRA, was said to have confessed the so-called discovery was a hoax intended to force Spanish authorities to cooperate by presenting them with a *fait accompli*. (Mrs. Asher later said in an interview that she had a tape recording of John

Sims denying that he had ever made such a statement to the *Newsweek* reporter.)

In Ireland, the embattled Maxine Asher dealt as best she could with phone calls from irate parents, rounded up the remnants of her team and library, and began explorations off the Irish coast and in the countryside near Galway and New Grange. They never found any conclusive evidence of Atlantis, but got some "strong feelings" that Ireland, Bimini, and other places in the Atlantic are all parts of a giant jigsaw puzzle that once was Atlantis. The program grew more and more impoverished until, at the end, they were eating what they could catch out of the Galway Bay, and Dr. Asher was doing all the cooking for the group.

Finally, back in Los Angeles at the end of August, Maxine Asher went about assessing her losses (some $75,000 of her own money), securing accreditation for the students who had gone on the trip, holding press conferences to "set the record straight," and, incredibly, planning her next Atlantean expedition. Admittedly, some of her allegations defy belief, yet she claims documentation to verify many of the accounts. She told the press that she and members of the group had been threatened, chased, and had their rooms broken into, and their mail tampered with while they were in Spain. She believed that the reason the expedition had failed was because of an international conspiracy involving all branches of government, economic interests, and the Hollywood motion picture industry, all of which, for various reasons, feared the outcome of her search. Nevertheless, there would be future expeditions, again based in Spain and Ireland but with possible side trips to such places as Egypt and the Basque country.

That was in 1973. Although one no longer hears very much about their Atlantean pursuits, Dr. Asher and members of her AMRA are still in the vanguard of intuitive archaeology. They have practiced their methods in the desert southwest and Ecuador and have trips planned to investigate ancient anthropology in several countries.

Dr. Asher reports that her office, museum, and library are based in Westwood, a Los Angeles suburb. Maxine Asher herself is adjunct professor with the University of San Francisco. She is advancing a project designed to search in Egypt for the missing records of Atlantis. Undaunted, she says that "what appeared to be a disastrous search for Atlantis in 1973 may actually have been the first breakthrough into ancient archaeology since Schliemann made his incredible discoveries at Troy . . ." Maxine Asher describes herself as "very clairvoyant" and says that "most of my discoveries are based initially on precognition." She says that she is "about 90 percent accurate" in these psychic functions but prefers to "work alone, because other people's vibrations cause interference." Her approach is probably best summarized with this observation: "I am constantly laboring in my research to validate the psychic approach in a scientific manner."

CHAPTER 13

Why "Atlantis"?

A lot of people who are fascinated by the idea that there was a continent, now lost, called Atlantis, are disenchanted when they hear that it might not have been located in the Atlantic Ocean. "After all," so their conscious or unconscious reasoning goes, "that's where it should have been!"

This unspoken argument often assumes that the Atlantic Ocean got its name, in the first place, from the legendary sunken Atlantis. Well, Atlantis and the Atlantic Ocean are certainly apples off the same linguistic tree. A Greek tree, as usual. *Atlantikos* originally referred to a sea beyond the mountains of Atlas—and Atlas, in Greek mythology, was the titan condemned to support the world, or at least the heavens, on his shoulders. In recent sculpture, Atlas usually holds up a globe symbolizing the earth. Homer wrote in the *Odyssey* that Atlas keeps the "tall pillars which hold heaven and earth asunder." (The first European maps used to show Atlas holding up the world on their covers, which is why we now call a collection of maps an "atlas.")

Greek mythology is confusing, at least when one looks back on it over the expanse of a few thousand years. When Plato talked about "Atlantis" as located beyond the "pillars of Hercules," he might have been talking about the pillars that Atlas was supposed to be holding up. At one point, Atlas and Hercules even changed places; Edith Hamilton summarizes this story delightfully in her *Mythology*. Hercules was enormously strong, kindly, but somewhat dim-witted. He was forever given virtually impossible tasks to perform (you've probably wondered how he cleaned the Augean stables, considering that Augeas had thousands of cattle and their stalls had not been cleared in years; well, Hercules simply diverted two rivers, made them run right through the stables and had the mess cleaned up in no time). But back to his encounter with Atlas. Among the many well-known "labors of Hercules" was the task of fetching the Golden Apples of Hesperides. Hercules didn't know where to find them, so he went to ask Atlas who was Hesperides' father. Dr. Hamilton writes:

"He [Hercules] offered to take upon himself the burden of the sky while Atlas was away [to get the golden apples]. Atlas, seeing a chance of being relieved forever from his heavy task, gladly agreed. He came back with the apples, but he did not give them to Hercules. He told Hercules he could keep on holding up the sky, for Atlas himself would take the apples to Eurystheus [who had asked for them in the first place]. On this occasion Hercules had only his wits to trust to: he had to give all his strength to supporting that mighty load. He was successful, but because of Atlas' stupidity rather than his own cleverness. He agreed to Atlas' plan, but asked him to take the sky back for just a moment so that Hercules could put a pad on his shoulders to ease the pressure. Atlas did so, and Hercules picked up the apples and went off."

Hercules, whose innumerable Superman-type exploits offer a mixture of tragedy and comedy, may have been a real person whose strength and adventures were exaggerated, embroidered, and mythologized. The pillars Plato mentions were probably, in his mind and those of his contemporaries, the ultimate point of the then known world. Just when the pillars of Hercules were identified as the Straits of Gibraltar, placing Atlantis in the Atlantic Ocean, cannot be determined; it may just have been the geopoetic imagination of a Renaissance writer—who thus spawned a legend superimposed upon a legend, in the long and great tradition of myth-making.

Plato may also have been writing about the so-called Islands of the Blessed, or Fortunate Island, a sort of Paradise archipelago inhabited by mortals on whom the gods had bestowed immortality. Map-makers of the Middle Ages used the name *Fortunatae insulae* for Madeira and the Canary Islands. Medieval writers didn't get the Atlantis legend directly from Plato but by way of Arabian geographers. Either during the Middle Ages or the Renaissance, the Atlas of Greek mythology gave his name to the Atlantic Ocean, as he had earlier done for Atlantis. The *Encyclopedia Britannica* blandly says that the term Atlantic Ocean "is supposedly derived from Atlantis, presumed to be a submerged continent below the present ocean."

It does take away a good deal of the charm and fascination of Atlantis to have to tear oneself away from the image of a huge continent—there seems to have been plenty of space for it—right in the middle of the Atlantic Ocean. Bits and pieces, such as the Azores (1,000 miles from the Europe, 2,000 miles from the American continent), look like logical remnants of such a continent, possible tops of very high mountains that signify a huge mountain range beneath. Modern oceanography has different ideas, as we shall see in later chapters. Meanwhile, once again, what did Plato and other ancient Greek writers really mean?

Homer, in his *Odyssey*, speaks of the legendary island of Ogygia and of Atlas' daughter, Calypso: "A Goddess inhabits this heavily forested Island; she is the Daughter of Atlas, who explores all that is Unknown, who knows the darkest deep of all oceans and who upholds by himself alone the giant pillars that keep earth and heaven apart." The ancient historian Herodotus refers in his fourth travel diary to the northwest corner of Africa and writes: "At last, after nearly ten days of travel, we reach another salt hill and an inhabited oasis. Next to the salt hill emerges a mountain with the name Atlas. It is a narrow mountain, rounded off, but believed to be quite high, so that its top is invisible, being cloud-covered in summer as well as winter. The people of the place say that it is actually a pillar that reaches into the sky."

The trick that Atlas is supposed to have played on Hercules, only to be trapped by the sly giant, was placed during a later version of Greek mythology at this very spot, the so-called Great Atlas range, with an average height of 11,000 feet. The people whom Herodotus quotes would have to be ancestors of Berber tribes. Two spots within this range, Cape Bon and Ceuta, have at one time or another been assumed to be the "Pillars of Hercules." They may well have been just that, at least in the minds of Greeks who knew their Plato and to whom, at a given period, these mountains were the outer limits of their known world. Incidentally, the very name Atlas Mountains was superimposed on the mountain chain, which runs pretty much parallel with the shore of northwest Africa, by Greeks or other inhabitants of the northern, opposite coast of the Mediterranean. The German scientist-writer Otto Muck maintains in *Alles über Atlantis* (1976) that the Atlas Mountains "received their name relatively late" and were known to local inhabitants originally either as Dyris or Daran. He adds: "The naming of the Ocean outside the 'Pillars of Hercules' as Atlantic—the very name of the Island—can be proven to be much earlier than this. The ocean could not have been named after the northwest African mountain. These mountains, and notably their main peak, were renamed, and Herodotus shows us why this happened." Muck maintains that the size of the mountain, its disappearance into the clouds, and its generally impressive appearance made it look very much like the *Ur*-Atlas, the original Atlas that disappeared into the Atlantic, together with the Island and all it contained. Muck maintains that the Azores provide "sparse relics", remnants of their one-time greatness.

Muck also writes: "The Island Atlantis, after which the Atlantic Ocean was named, received its own name from a Great Mountain that dominated it and served as a giant landmark." When Atlantis disappeared, the German writer suggests, "the original image was recovered," transferred to the Atlas Mountains, and thus "the mythical symbol was recreated."

CHAPTER 14

Edgar Cayce's Atlantis "Readings"

Have we lived before? Perhaps in ancient Egypt, Greece, or Rome—or perhaps even in that legendary origin of all these civilizations, the Lost Continent of Atlantis? The idea of having lived on Atlantis, or its Indian Ocean equivalent, Lemuria (the Lost Continent of Mu) has undoubted fascination to every one of us. Through clairvoyants, automatic writings, or visions with or without drugs, thousands of people throughout the world have come to the conclusion that they have passed through many previous incarnations and will be reincarnated yet again, and again.

Of all reincarnation versions, whether phantasy or reality, the Atlantis concept is somehow the most intriguing. One "astral clairvoyant," W. Scott-Elliot, claimed in his book *The Story of Atlantis,* published in the 1890s, that Atlanteans existed more than a million years ago. He wrote that they included black aboriginals, 10 to 12 feet tall, who were enslaved by the Toltecs, who averaged eight feet in height.

According to Scott-Elliot, the Toltecs resorted to black magic, and as retribution a volcanic cataclysm sank Atlantis. This, he said, was 200,000 years ago; the Toltecs migrated to Egypt and took their advanced technological civilization with them. Their descendants migrated to other regions, including Central America, the Middle East, and parts of Europe; pyramid-building was among their skills. There are similarities between this version and the work of Ignatius Donnelly, as well as of others who claimed to have received their information from "higher sources," presumably by automatic writing or auditory messages of a more or less hallucinatory nature.

The most detailed body of fairly contemporary writings on Atlantis as the stage for previous incarnations comes from Edgar Cayce, the seer who gave 14,246 "readings" between 1901 and 1945. These statements were usually given to men or women seeking advice for their health or careers, and were designed to find clues to present problems—and their solutions—in events during earlier incarnations. The readings were given by Cayce in a trancelike state or sleep, during which he spoke in a rather convuluted way, using a special vocabulary; the person for whom the reading was designed, for example, was usually referred as the "entity."

If one pieces together the scattered bits of Atlantis information that emerged from Cayce's individual readings, they form a mosaic of uneven design. He referred to earlier Atlantean incarnations in the lives of 664 people to whom he spoke. If one wonders where Atlantis was located, he can be found to have named three specific locations: (1) Off the Florida coast, where the island of Bimini is now located; (2) In the temple records "that were in Egypt"; and (3) on the Mexican peninsula of Yucatán, where there existed "these stones" which he called "the Emblem of same," to be brought to the United States, "the Pennsylvania State Museum," to "the Washington preservations," or "to Chicago." The Cayce readings suggested that three separate catastrophic upheavals destroyed Atlantis, each lasting months or years: the first in 50,700 B.C., the second in 28,000 B.C.—at which point the Continent was splintered by cosmic rays into several separate islands, of which the major one was called Poseidia. Cayce said that the final destruction took place about 10,000 B.C., and this has been interpreted as the cataclysm referred to by Plato.

Atlantean spirit beings, Cayce suggested, first made their appearance on earth, as souls or thought forms. They were known as the Sons of the Law of One, but selfishness and greed drove some to manifest themselves materially in order to experience a state of sense consciousness.

According to Cayce, they were one of five nations that "landed" on earth. He associates the number five, in the Hindu manner, as *Prakriti*—the five *gunas*—or five senses: "When the earth brought forth the seed in her season, and man came in the earth plane as the lord of that in that sphere, man appeared in five places then at once—the five senses, the five reasons, the five spheres, the five developments, the five nations. Of which Atlantis was the most advanced." He approximates their location to have been between the Gulf of Mexico and the Mediterranean. "Evidences of this lost civilization are to be found in the Pyrenees and Morocco, British Honduras, Yucatan and America . . . especially or notably, in Bimini and in the Gulf Stream through this vicinity . . ." The five races to begin life on earth were yellow, white, red (Atlantean and American Indian), brown, and black. Portions of Atlantis existed as long as 10 million years ago, but not in a physical form.

Cayce suggested that this came about in order to know the five senses and gradually took on the form we see today as representing man. They opposed God's will to remain spiritual beings and chose the world of the flesh. Following the animal pattern, they separated into male and female and apparently had intercourse with animals. The creatures born of them, he tells us, were "things" they used as slaves. Those who held fast to their spiritual birthright were known as the Sons of the Law of One. Those who sought sensual pleasures and other selfish desires became locked into the material forms they had created for their sensory experiences. Eventually, they could no longer move freely in and out of their material bodies. They became known as the Sons of Belial, and like the animal, also experienced death and rebirth.

Edgar Cayce describes the children of the Law of One in a reading for someone whom he identifies in that lifetime as Rhea: "Throughout that particular period of experiences in Atlantis, the children of the Law of One—were giving periods to the concentration of thought for the use of the universal forces, through the guidance or direction of the saints (as would be termed today).

"There are few terms in the present that would indicate the state of consciousness; save that, through the concentration of the group mind of the children of the Law of One, they entered into a fourth-dimensional consciousness—or were absent from the body." It seems they thought as a group rather than as individuals; Cayce referring to the Belial people spoke of, "individuals and material things for self-aggrandizement or indulgence without due consideration for the freedom of choice or decision by those who were then, in a physical experience, in that state of evolution of developing their mental abilities for single or separate activity."

The "things" or offspring of Belial he describes as follows: "Those individuals who had through their sojourns in the earth as souls pushed into matter as to become separate entities, without the consideration of principle or the ability of self-control, might be compared to the domestic pets of to-day—as the present development of the horse, the mule, the dog, the cat." Here Cayce assures us that he does not mean transmigration of souls from animal to human; yet, the Belial people took on the form of animals apparently, or, at least, through intercourse created creatures that originated in SOUL . . . . were these not of the origin of God? Were the Belials not brothers to the spiritual beings? At any rate, the war that was to plague them for thousands of years was over the monstrous offspring that the Sons of Belial abused and mistreated. The spiritual beings sought to help the creatures Cayce calls the "sons of men" to develop their spirituality and free them from bondage. But sex had become the preoccupation of the Belial people and a slow war began between the now divided but once pure spiritual beings. The Sons of the Law of One created *man*; through this form they might be better able to communicate with and help those who had strayed, enable them to regain their true state and reunite with God. This is linked to the phrase in *Genesis*, "Let us make man in our image . . ." Though the Belials had departed from their divine origin, they still possessed the same powers and built a great "firestone" with which to regenerate their bodies and prevent death. This stone also supplied them with power to operate their ships, planes, and all energy sources.

The animals began invading the earth at a rapid rate. In an attempt to control overpopulation, explosives were used which resulted in volcanic eruptions and the eventual collapse of Atlantis.

They were, according to Cayce, a highly technical civilization, advanced in the uses of atomic energy. The explosives, he tells us, "were not only the rays from the sun, set by the facets of the stones as crystallized from the heat from within the elements of the earth itself, but were as the combinations of these . . . The use of these influences by the Sons of Belial brought, then, the first of the upheavals; or the turning of the etheric rays' influence *from* the sun—as used by the Sons of the Law of One—into the facet for the activities of same—produced . . . a volcanic upheaval . . ."

The date was 50,700 B.C.

The exodus began in South and Central America, Egypt, Spain, and Portugal. What happened during this time we are not told, but the fact that the two groups continued their battle over the "things" seems unchanged by their migration.

In 28,000 B.C. the next cataclysm occurs, this time by accidently tuning up their energy plant too high. He refers to it as a "firestone." In one reading we find: "About the firestone that was in the experience did the activities of the entity then make those applications that dealt with both the constructive and destructive forces in the period."

Cayce said that, "both constructive and destructive forces were generated by the activity of this stone." He specified: "In the center of a building, that today would be said to have been lined with non-conductive metals, or non-conductive stone—something akin to asbestos, with ... other non-conductors that are now being manufactured in England under a name that is known well to many of those that deal in such things.

"The building above the stone was oval, or a dome wherein there could be or was the rolling back, so that the activity of the stone was received from the sun's rays, or from the stars; the concentrating of the energies that emanate from bodies that are fire themselves—with the elements that are found and that are not found in the earth's atmosphere. The concentration through the prisms or glass, as would be called in the present, was in such a manner that it acted upon the instruments that were connected with the various modes of travel, through induction methods—that made much the character of control as the remote control through radio vibrations or directions would be in the present day; though the manner of the force that was impelled from the stone acted upon the motivating forces in the crafts themselves.

"There was the preparation so that when the dome was rolled back there might be little or no hindrance in the application direct to the various crafts that were to be impelled through space, whether in the radius of the visioning of the one eye, as it might be called, or whether directed under water or under other elements or through other elements.

"The preparation of this stone was in the hands only of the initiates at the time, and the entity was among those that directed the influences of the radiation that arose in the form of the rays that were invisible to the eye but that acted upon the stones themselves as set in the motivating forces— whether the aircraft that were lifted by the gases in the period or whether guiding the more pleasure vehicles that might pass along close to the earth, or what would be termed the crafts on the water or under the water.

"These, then, were impelled by the concentrating of the rays from the stone that was centered in the middle of the power station, or power house (that would be termed in the present).

"In the active forces of these the entity brought destructive forces, by the setting up—in various portions of the land—the character that was to act as producing the powers in the various forms of the people's activities in the cities, the towns, the countries surrounding same. These, not intentionally, were *tuned* too high—and brought the second period of destructive forces to the peoples in the land, and broke up the land into the isles that later became the periods when the further destructive forces were brought in the land. . . . At first, it was not the intention nor desire for destructive forces. Later it was for the ascension of power itself.

"As to describing the manner of construction of the stone, we find it was a large cylindrical glass (as would be termed today), cut with facets in such a manner that the capstone on top of same made for the centralizing of the power or force that concentrated between the end of the cylinder and the capstone itself.

"As indicated, the records of the manners of construction of same are in three places in the earth, as it stands today. In the sunken portions of Atlantis, or Poseidia, where a portion of the temples may yet be discovered, under the slime of ages of sea water—near what is known as Bimini, off the coast of Florida. And in the temple records that were in Egypt, where the entity [the person to whom this message was addressed] later acted in cooperation with others in preserving the records that came from the land where these had been kept. Also the records that were carried to what is now Yucatán in America, where these stones (that they know so little about) are now—during the last few months—*being* uncovered . . ."

The second period of destruction triggered by cosmic rays splintered the land into islands—five in number. Many migrated to America in Nevada and Colorado. Those that remained continued to flourish and to battle over the material versus the spiritual.

The third and final destruction that ends this bizarre story came at the time alluded to by Plato. Of the 133 million Atlantean souls many "set sail for the Egyptian land, but entered rather into the Pyrenees and what is now the Portuguese, French and Spanish land. And there *still* may be seen in the chalk cliffs there in Calais ... where the marks of the entity's followers were made, as the attempts were set ... to create a temple activity to the follower of the Law of One ... first to begin the establishment of the library of knowledge in Alexandria; ten thousand three hundred [years] before the Prince of Peace ..."

Now, this Cayce "revelation" will remain myth or hypothesis until marine archaeology has found proof for it on ocean floors. But much of what Cayce said as to the age of man, and the locations where indications might be found, has gained increased attention. His readings were given from 1923 to 1944. Atomic energy did not go into production until 1942.

Until 1960, the oldest human was believed to be the 300,000- to 500,000-year-old Java/Peking man, but in that year, Dr. L. S. B. Leakey discovered the Zinjanthropus—age 600,000 years—in Olduvai Gorge in Tanzania, Africa. Three years later, he found another man called Homo habilis, believed to be 1,850,000 years old. But Dr. Johannes Heurezeler of Basle University, Switzerland, found a complete skeleton hundreds of feet deep in an Italian coal mine. His conclusion was that it was definitely a humanoid classified as a 10 million-year-old man. Modern animals and plants in remarkably well-preserved condition were near the fossil, and all were found to be of the same age. Such animals and plants were not known to exist in that time—yet there they were. This bridges the agricultural gap between the Old and the New Worlds.

In Nevada, another alleged corner of the Atlantean civilization, tools of men were found along with a variety of animal bones in Tule Springs. The age as determined by W. F. Libby is 23,800 years. Another location cited by Cayce has harbored on the island of Santa Rosa (off the coast of California) buried bones believed to be around 29,650 years old. Many more locations have produced evidence of man's existence in parts of the world Cayce referred to as being Atlantean.

The battle of good and evil will continue among the reincarnated souls who certainly make up our population in number—Cayce foretold—and the holocausts and earth changes will be repeated unless we give up our Belial heritage and return once more to the Law of One: "As to the changes physical again: The earth will be broken up in the western portion of America. The greater portion of Japan must go into the sea. The upper portion of Europe will be changed as in the twinkling of an eye. Land will appear off the east coast of America. There will be the upheavals in the Arctic and in the Antarctic that will make for the eruption of volcanoes in the Torrid areas, and there will be shifting then of the poles—so that where there has been those of a frigid or the semitropical will become the more tropical, and moss and fern will grow. And these will begin in those periods in '58 to '98 when these will be proclaimed as the periods when His light will be seen again in the clouds."

In 1932 when he gave these readings, he zeroed in on America: New York City will disappear, southern portions of Carolina and Georgia will vanish overnight. The Great Lakes will flow into the Gulf of Mexico . . . Safety lands will be Virginia Beach, where the Cayce foundation is now located; portions of Ohio, Indiana, Illinois, and much of the southern and eastern portions of Canada.

Cayce has been on target many times. For example, the Dead Sea Scrolls were discovered 11 years after he gave a reading on the incarnation of a woman who had been a member of the Essene community at the exact spot where the scrolls were found. And more, in 1936, at the time of the reading, historical references indicated that these were communities of men only. Excavations 15 years later produced skeletons of *women* as well as men.

Salome, a Biblical figure that Cayce said in a 1939 reading had been present at the death and raising of Lazarus, was referred to in a manuscript discovered in 1960 at the Monastery of Mar Saba near Jerusalem. An ancient letter believed written by St. Mark, narrates the miracle of Lazarus, and a woman named Salome is introduced as being present.

Edgar Cayce's complex drama of the Atlanteans is baffling as history, fascinating to those who envision their own previous incarnations during one of several of the Atlantis evolutions. But, at least in the case of his reference to remnants of the Lost Continent near the Caribbean island of Bimini, Cayce's description has had at least partial confirmation. The search for Atlantis near Bimini is on!

CHAPTER 15

Bimini's "Sacred Geometry"

Edgar Cayce, as we have seen not only predicted the discovery of Atlantis but suggested a specific location: "A portion of the temple may yet be discovered under the slime of ages of sea water—near what is known as Bimini, off the coast of Florida." A few years later Cayce predicted a discovery date: "And Poseidia will be among the first portions of Atlantis to rise again. Expect it in sixty-eight and sixty-nine. Not so far away!"

Not so far away in time or place—Bimini is only a morning's sail from Miami, across the Florida Strait. In 1956, some marble columns were observed, standing upright in 60 feet of water. Two years later, Dr. William Bell of Marion, North Carolina, photographed a "six-foot column or spire protruding from a double circular gearlike base embedded in the ocean floor." The photographs, Robert Ferro and Michael Grumley report in their book, *Atlantis: The Autobiography of A Search* (1970), exhibit "peculiar emanations of light from the base of the shaft." Their fisherman guide Evangelo knew of the column, which he said Bimini guides had used as a fishing marker until sand buried it.

A decade later, and just in time to fulfill Cayce's prediction, the Bimini sands parted to reveal other finds. In 1967, Dimitri Rebikoff, an expert in underwater photography and optics, saw from the air a rectangular area in the sea north of Andros Island, Bahama. In 1968, Trigg Adams and Robert Brush, pilots who were also members of the Cayce organization, the Association for Research and Enlightenment (ARE), saw it too. Dr. J. Manson Valentine, a zoologist and searcher for lost culture, examined the find. He described the structure, standing in about six feet of water, as "the first of its kind in the western hemisphere" and speculated that it might be a temple. "The top," he reported in the Rome *Daily*

American article that sparked Ferro and Grumley's search, "is about two feet above the ocean floor. The walls are sloping . . . The material is a kind of masonry and it is definitely man-made."

Some were immediately reminded of Cayce's prediction of a temple to be found near Bimini. They found a remarkable similarity between its floor plan and that of the "Temple of the Turtles" in Uxmal, Yucatán. Cayce had predicted, after all, that "evidences of Atlantean civilization" might be found "in British Honduras, Yucatán, and parts of the Americas—especially near Bimini and in the Gulf Stream in this vicinity."

Aerial photographs taken by Trigg Adams showed several submerged formations in the "temple" waters. Had the undersea remains of some prehistoric city indeed been found? Or, as others suggested, was the construction a Spanish fort, a sponge concentration, or a fish trap? No one quite knew. But Charles Berlitz, who collaborated with Dr. Valentine to produce the book *Mysteries from Forgotten Worlds,* thought it likely that they were buildings constructed on dry land which later sank or was inundated by a rising sea.

In September, 1968, Dr. Valentine, working with Rebikoff and Jacques Mayol, a record-holding diver, found more rocks. This time, it was a formation of huge stone blocks about a thousand yards from the shore of North Bimini. This pavement, as Dr. Valentine described it in an article for *Muse News,* the Miami Museum of Science's publication, ran for 1,800 feet roughly parallel to the shore.

Late the same fall, Robert Ferro and Michael Grumley set out from Manasquan Inlet in their 37-foot cruiser *Tana.* By February, 1969, they had been introduced to Dr. Valentine in Miami and had crossed the Florida Straits to Bimini. With Valentine and others from the Marine Archeological Research Society aboard, they sailed the *Tana* up the west coast of North Bimini to a spot about three-quarters of a mile off Paradise Point. Here the guide Evangelo indicated some uncovered rocks lay beneath the waves. Ferro and Grumley jumped in immediately and then surfaced to tell the others that they were anchored above a "wide wall or road-bed," with rocks as large as 18 to 20 feet long and 10 feet wide. They estimated the formation to be about 700 yards long. Ferro and Valentine both took photos, and Ferro chipped off a sample from one of the smaller stones.

Dr. Valentine theorized on the boat that the find might be a Sac Bey or White Road like those found in Yucatán. Ferro and Grumley, and later Count Pino Turolla, preferred to think of it as a sea wall or dike. In March, Count Turolla photographed the formation and brought up a small rock which, when dried, "had a metallic sound when struck" and which, he was advised by Carl Holm, the president of Global Oceanics, was apparently not native to Bimini or the Bahamas.

Other expeditions and finds followed. Count Turolla discovered three more sections of the wall-like formation, one about 80 yards long off North Bimini and two others off South Bimini. Because the last section appears to turn eastward around the tip of South Bimini, Turolla believes that the formation may encircle both islands. Turolla also located and photographed groups of pillars. "The visible sections of these pillars," he wrote to Ferro and Grumley, "varied in length between three to five feet and the diameter betwoon two to three feet. . . . On the last trip, November 29, 1969, we were able to secure part of one pillar for closer examination. Subsequent analysis and opinion from experts is that the composition of the sample pillar is not domestic stone from the Bahamian banks or man-made material but, rather, seems to have been carved from natural stone, perhaps from South America."

Dimitri Rebikoff, using his "Pegasus" underwater platform and a special corrective lens, produced a stereoscopic mosaic of the center south wall, which showed large blocks of limestone in a pattern reminiscent of Roman paving stones. Rebikoff also photographed from the air other unusually shaped underwater formations off the Bahama Banks and found a wall built around a freshwater spring in the ocean.

Other finds reported by Charles Berlitz in the area included mangrove roots on one of the walls which could, according to carbon-14 dating, be 6,000 to 12,000 years old and a possible temple platform in deep water off the Bahama Banks. Reports circulate of an undersea marble acropolis four or five acres in extent and of fluted columns raised on pillars in the fashion of Mediterranean dock buildings.

The reticence of the Bimini searchers in pinpointing their

discoveries, which would normally be very suspect in scientific circles, is less so in this case. Underwater archaeology is plagued by souvenir-hunting amateur divers. Two thousand-year-old wrecks in the Mediterranean have been stripped of their invaluable cargoes by such divers in a single season. Thus the vagueness of the locations and descriptions of the Bimini finds, while frustrating to those trying to verify them, is understandable, particularly in an area where scuba diving is a popular sport.

John Gifford, a graduate student of the Division of Marine Geology, University of Miami, directed an expedition in 1970 to survey the formations off Paradise Point. He returned in 1971 with George Lindstrom, president of the Washington, D.C., Scientific Exploration and Archeological Society (SEAS), sponsored by the University of Miami and the National Geographic Society. In 1972 Gifford and Lindstrom made a third survey. In 1974, Dr. David Zink, a professor of English at Lamar University, Beaumont, Texas, spent five weeks diving, photographing, and taking fathometer profiles over the Paradise Point site. He also investigated an area to the east of Bimini that some believe may have been an ancient reservoir. Dr. Zink reported his findings in an article, "The Search for Atlantis Continues" in *The A.R.E. Journal* (Vol. X, No. 3, May, 1975).

The true significance of these formations remains controversial. They are hard to study, for they are often covered by bottom sands within a few months of their discovery. Dr. John E. Hall, an associate professor of archaeology from the University of Miami and a member of the 1970 expedition, believes that these stones "constitute a natural phenomenon called pleistocene beachrock erosion and cracking." He observed "no evidence whatsoever of any work of human hand or any kind of engineering."

John Gifford was not so sure; he found it strange that the stresses which produced cracking in these formations had not produced it in other areas. He noted that the blocks could not be correlated with other rock types in the vicinity. "None of the evidence," he wrote, "disproves human intervention on their formation." But in an article a few months later in a scholarly publication, he called the Bimini rocks "a natural beach-rock deposit."

Dr. David Zink had access to Gifford's field survey and

Hall's article and was briefed by Dr. Valentine before setting out to survey the Bimini area. He came away from five weeks of exploration convinced that the site was archaeological and not natural. The blocks, he found, are not attached to the sea floor, are of different thicknesses, and of square and rectangular shapes. Micrite in composition, rather than the soft oolite of beachrock in the Bahamas, they do not slope as does beachrock in the area.

During the summer of 1975, a second expedition took place. As reported by Dr. Zink under the title "Poseida 75: A Progress Report," which appeared in *The A.R.E. Journal* (Vol. XI, No. 3, May, 1976), two auxiliary sloops were used to explore the Bimini area, the *Makai II* and the *Gypsy*. Zink, by now on a sabbatical leave from Lamar University, used his personal skill as a scuba diver and his blue-water sailing experience. While about a dozen people were on the two boats, others were quartered ashore at the Bimini apartment of writer Peter Tompkins. In other words, some 20 people were involved in the venture, including divers, archaeologists, a marine biologist, geologists, a cartographer, and—in line with a new trend in parapsychological archaeology—a psychic; indeed, psychic skills that seem to involve dowsing, clairvoyance, or a mixture of ESP abilities have recently been utilized by archaeologists with apparently significant results. The psychic who helped the 1975 Bimini expedition was Ms. Carol Hufstickler, who had previously been a subject of the dream telepathy experiments at the Maimonides Clinic's Dream Laboratory, Brooklyn, N.Y., under the direction of Dr. Stanley Krippner.

The expedition concentrated on defining the nature of an undersea "road" northwest of North Bimini. Is this formation, they asked, of a natural geological nature—or is it man-made? Zink wrote that the findings confirm Dr. J. Manson Valentine's claim that it is, in fact, "a man-made formation of the type usually known as megalithic," which "places it in the same category of constructions as the pre-Incan parts of Sacsahuamán in Peru, Tiahuanaco in Bolivia, Stonehenge in England and Carnac in Brittany."

Zink adds that such sites, of which Stonehenge is the best known, have been identified with "significant astronomical and terrestrial alignment," and have been called "sacred geometry." He adds that "the survey done by Poseidia 75 also uncovered evidence which points toward a sacred geometry contained within the Bimini site." This included "one crucial star alignment" and "a solar star alignment seems to be present," although this will need further confirmation. Zink reminds us that underwater sites cannot be calculated as to age, the way we've learned to do with archaeological sites on dry land. Tidal currents play havoc with known measuring techniques.

The expedition compared the structure of the Bimini "road" with similar underwater phenomena in the area. They concluded that here, indeed, were stones of a nature and dimensions that strongly suggested architectual skill; at three points, they observed structures "in which stones were stacked three high," and often one of the larger stones of the "road" was on top. Many smaller clues convinced the expedition that the evidence it found "points more toward man-made construction than a natural geological feature."

Zink asked, "If it is an archaeological site, what is its function?" It should just be called a "road," he suggests. Perhaps it was part of a harbor. Or, because it may originally have been horseshoe-shaped (its remnants look like a "J"), it bears similarity to the "megalithic sacred sites of Europe," such as Stonehenge. That doesn't mean the Bimini structure needs to be part of the same culture, but that, as Zink puts it, "its dominant function" may have been "a sacred use"— which leads him back to the concept of "sacred geometry." Zink says the structure seems to favor a 90-degree orientation, "the solar alignment of the equinoxes, hinting at a solar cult." Also, "the dramatic arrangement of the stones themselves" gives clues pointing toward sacred geometry.

Future expeditions will dig for pottery or other artifacts that will permit dating of the site. Zink says that "6,000 B.C. is a reasonable date for its last human occupancy." He found a stone building fragment "with a sophisticated tongue-and-groove joint system" of a composition "not native to the Bahamas." He says it has "been estimated to be at least 3,000 years old." One of the expedition's divers, Garry Varney, found "a stylized marble head with a heavily eroded surface," over 300 pounds in weight. Identification of both items will be a considerable challenge.

Not too long ago, the idea of sunken harbors and cities brought knowing smiles to the faces of orthodox geologists and archaeologists. They were convinced that the level of the sea had remained unchanged for at least 10,000 years, and that the widespread stories of sunken cities current among coastal peoples on both sides of the Atlantic were no more than myths and legends. More recently, studies in the Mediterranean and the North Sea have made it plain that the sea level has fluctuated quite markedly even in historic times.

Variations in sea level have three possible causes. They can be due to eustatic change—a rise in the oceans due to glacial melting. Tectonic change—earthquakes and volcanic activity—can raise or lower the sea level in a particular area. And isostatic movements—the result of stresses due to formation or melting of glaciers, or to the shifting weight of land and water masses—can alter sea level.

During the last Ice Age, the sea level probably dropped about 200 meters, 600 feet, below its present level. Vast areas of the continental shelves, including most of the area around the Bahamas, would then have been dry land. The continental shelf extends widely off Yucatán, Central America, and the northern coast of South America. Possibly man could once walk, and transport stones, from South or Central America to the Bahamas.

How old could the Bimini finds be? Dr. Valentine guessed them to date from 8,000 to 10,000 B.C. That's probably the last time Bimini was above sea level. But we can't be sure. The towns of Jamestown, on Nevis, and Orangetown, on St. Eustatius, sank into the ocean following an earthquake on April 30, 1680, and now lie in water ranging up to 20 meters deep. Port Royal, Jamaica, slipped under the sea in an earthquake on June 7, 1692. The controversial theories of Dr. Immanuel Velikovsky assume recent and catastrophic changes in earth's surface resulting from near-collisions with the moon or other heavenly bodies. Those theories are being reexamined. A more recent date for the subsidence of the Bimini site could be possible.

How old are the prehistoric constructions of Latin America? Some estimates for the age of the vast ruined city Tiahuanaco range as high as 15,000 years. More conservative dates for some of these cyclopean constructions might range in the vicinity of 2000 B.C. The proto-harbors of the Mediterranean could also be as old as that. It's fascinating to speculate that the peoples who built the second might have seen, or even constructed, the first. Could related peoples have constructed a sea wall, a temple, or some more mysterious structure on the Bimini shore? Could the seeds of the Atlantis story have sprung from tales of trans-Atlantic voyages garbled and distorted in the telling? More diving, more scraping, more pulling, hauling, and calculations will be necessary before these questions may even be partially answered.

CHAPTER 16

The Once and Future Paradise

Atlantis retains and renews its hold on our imagination, because its image responds to a lasting human need: the belief in an ideal world, an example we hope to emulate. Plato, who dropped the Atlantis image into the pool of memory of our civilization, was himself a dreamer of fantastic dreams. His *Republic* envisioned order and beauty in human culture but it demanded an authoritarianism we have come to know all too well in this century—and without which his utopian society could not survive.

And why not? Why can't we have a free utopian society? And was not Atlantis, whatever we know of it, such a society?

Plato's ship of dreams foundered on the reality of human nature. His ideal society could only be maintained as a police state; in our day, it would have to be a computerized version of ancient Sparta or, at one point, of ancient Crete—part of the very Atlantis we now perceive in retrospect. And, to answer the last question, the Atlantis of Plato, the ancient Crete with its delightful Minoan civilization, could not truly have been the dream society we imagine.

The Atlantis that succumbed to the sea-and-earthquake of antiquity, whose palaces, homes, and shops of artisans burned down and were covered with ashes, does not emerge from the mist of time as the paradisical place that Plato and his successors have described. Yet, in bare outlines, the Plato version may well have been correct. Allowing for the patina of many centuries, and the poetic version Plato gave us in retrospect, Cretan Atlantis was a society of high standards, of affluence, art, and beauty. We cannot be sure at exactly what point of its development this Aegean Atlantis succumbed to tidal waves, earthquake, and fire. But if modern archaeology is anywhere close in its estimates, disaster hit this island very near the pinnacle of its existence.

Atlantis may well be seen as an expression of two apparently quite contradictory drives within man's unconscious: a desire for paradisical perfection and a fascination with catastrophe.

On the one hand, we all desire the innocence and paradisical nature of the Garden of Eden; on the other hand, we seem to revel in, and even hope for, disaster. It is a simple psychological guess, and quite a good guess at that, that the millennia-old fascination with Atlantis lies in the fact that, as fact or legend, it accomodates these apparently diametrically opposed drives. It doesn't make sense, in everyday terms of practicality, to be attracted by opposites. And yet, let us look around and see whether we do not find mini-Atlantis patterns in the world familiar to us.

As examples, certain modern sports events will do very well—and we should remember that ancient Minoa, setting of Atlantis, knew their equivalent. The bullfight has come down to us directly from the encounters with a bull we see depicted on vases and frescoes of ancient Crete. The crowd urges on the bullfighter, it adores him, women desire him; but if he is gored, if the bull turns on him, the crowd is even more thrilled by the spectacle of blood, danger, injury, and possible death. The Mediterranean bullfight tradition, which has its foothold in the western hemisphere in Mexico, has other regional equivalents. Most striking in its external contrasts, because of the element of technology, is the motor car race. The great races of our day, ranging from the Indianapolis 500 to the Monte Carlo Rallye, are crowd-pleasers precisely because they contain all the psychodynamic elements of the bullfight.

Racing driver and matador are made of the same material, in character and unconscious drive. The racing crowd includes its aficionados, its erotically involved "groupies," as does the bullfight mob. The supermasculine element of provoking danger has been dramatized in many forms by writers who themselves sought or seek identification with virility, high risk, the danger of death. Ernest Hemingway's name comes to mind most easily, because he represented a generation of men who sought fulfillment in daring and defying death. Hemingway killed himself, rather than wait for natural death to catch up with him.

Is Atlantis then, in the human mind, essentially no more and no less than a super-bullfight?

Of course, it isn't as simple as that. The legend of Atlantis presents a glorious Eden that was devoured by water and fire, by earth and sea quakes, possibly by envious or avenging divinities. The image of a flourishing civilization, perhaps "better"—in whatever way—than our own, vanishing overnight has much of the fascination that we see constantly expressed in motion pictures that depict earthquakes, the sinking of a ship while its passengers are in the midst of revelry, the inferno of an office building that is devoured by a mass of fire, the exaggerated danger from the sea that a shark might represent, the horrors of supernatural forces overcoming us from outer space or other dimensions.

Psychologists are not sure just why young children have a voracious appetite for horror movies and stories and pictures of monsters. Is it because these are dangers that are obviously outside the realm of the real and possible? Are these monsters safely caged, as it were, on the screen of the motion picture theater or the television set? Yes, probably; but they also act as a channel for a child's, or an adult's own aggression—he can identify alternately with the "good guy" or the villain, be horrified and titillated at the same time.

The image of a whole continent being swallowed up by the sea, which has been the standard version of "the last days of Atlantis" in much of the literature on the subject, is close to the ultimate in horror. It is odd, therefore, that modern psychology has paid no attention whatever to unconscious elements that have obviously kept the Atlantis legend so vividly alive. Along the pattern of the thoughts advanced by the founder of psychoanalysis, Dr. Sigmund Freud, fascination with Atlantis as a version of man's "Lost Paradise" can be interpreted as the unending desire to return to mother's womb, to the total perfection of being sustained without exertion or responsibility. That, crudely put, would be a Freudian explanation for the lush variety of Garden of Eden myths that filled the hope, the poetry, and the myths of mankind throughout its recorded history.

Other Freudian elements can also be applied to the two-sided fascination with Atlantis. But Freud himself did not refer to Atlantis in his own voluminous writing. And what is even more startling, Dr. C. G. Jung, the Swiss philosopher who founded the school of analytical psychology, also did not seek to find a link between Atlantis fascination and what he called the "archetypal" elements in man's unconscious. Only very briefly, in a paper entitled "A Psychological Approach to the Dogma of the Trinity," did Jung refer to Plato's description of Atlantis. He suggested that Plato had been trying to "bring forth the mandala structure that later appeared as the capital of Atlantis in his *Critias*." The mandala plays a key role in Jung's view that man's collective unconscious develops certain basic motifs, of which the mandala, an intricately designed circular painting or sculpture, is perhaps the major artistic expression.

Others, more recently, have dealt with our apparently continuing need for myths on a more contemporary level. *The New York Times*, in a series of interviews with psychologists (July 4, 1976) on a related subject, elicited a number of responses that reached more or less the same conclusion: we need myth, because our realities are too rigid and confining. Dr. Gertrude Williams, a St. Louis psychologist, was quoted as saying that such myths "represent an existential desire to get beyond the real, drab, predictable, plastic world." She added: "Just as there may be a fear of the unknown, there is embedded in the human psyche a wish for the unknown, a desire to explore the offbeat."

But is it quite enough to observe and state what, at least to our generation, has become the obvious? Is it sufficient to state that man, at this stage of his evolution, still thrills to the idea of Paradise Found and Paradise Destroyed?

Let us search for an answer to this question in the gigantic, efficient, often hugely commercially successful trends in filmmaking. Television has driven the cinema manufacturers into ever deeper, ever more primitive, ever more ambitious safaris into the basic elements in mass psychology—mass needs, mass fears, mass desires. The version of Atlantis that we have inherited from the prodigious, multifaceted Ignatius Donnelly will not leave us alone—it persists, and it has had a minor parallel within the relatively recent past. The most dramatic was the sinking of the ocean liner, the *Titanic*, on April 14, 1912. The ship struck an iceberg, sank within three hours, and more than 1,500 of its over 2,200 passengers and crew members drowned. Not long ago, a fictionalized version of this event, *The Poseidon Adventure*, became a highly successful motion picture—one of a long and continuing line of disaster exploitation films.

The sinking of the *Titanic*, in terms of mass psychology, was a miniature Atlantis. The major elements were identical. But, above all, there was the image of a society—the supposedly highly developed one of the island, and that of the champagne-drinking passengers of the luxury liner—being swallowed up by the all-devouring sea. The image stands for more, I think, than our fascination with Paradise Found and Paradise Destroyed. The *Titanic* was the prime product of a self-assured, even arrogant pre-World War I civilization. The ship had been reported to be unsinkable; ancient Greek mythologists would have immediately seen such a claim of dangerous human *hubris* as a challenge to jealous or vindictive gods.

Somehow, the horrified readers of news about the *Titanic* disaster, way down in their unacknowledged jungle of personal envy, may well have thought, "It served them right." And beyond that: "I wasn't one of them, the High and Mighty Ones, with their pearls and dinner dresses, their drinking and dancing—and I was spared, in my humble existence!" The sinking of the *Titanic*, like the legend of Atlantis, harks back—as Donnelly rightly noted—to the biblical flood. God had found mankind sinful and decided to wipe it out, except for two of each species, to start all over again. The wages of sin were death by water, by drowning; water covers, purifies, renews.

The rite of Baptism embraces this element of purification in its earliest and simplest form. Without it, the infant is considered to be still impure: Original Sin clings to its body and its soul. Beyond this, the baptismal rite is one of exorcism, immunization against invasion by demons or evil spirits. The water washes away the sins of the past and immunizes against the sins of the future, or at least their temptation.

All this is virtually virgin territory in the literature of psychology, although the concept of "mythopoesis" has been explored by at least one noted U.S. psychoanalyst, Dr. Harry Slochower, editor of *The American Imago*, a journal devoted to the psychological study of culture, science, and the arts. Slochower notes that the revival of a myth in our time "is an attempt to satisfy the human need for relatedness to fellow-travelers on our common journey," including civilizations that have preceded our own. In mythic language, he says, "the problems deal with Creation, with Destiny, with the Quest" of man. The theme of apocalyptic vision, so essential to a modern view of the Atlantis legend—now that we may have physically encountered remnants of its origins—is an ever-vivid drama of human nature and action.

Dr. Joost A. M. Meerloo writes in *Creativity and Externization* that "we hate and we love destruction," noting "man's contrasting attitudes toward danger and catastrophe." He sees "behind the display of horror, our primitive megalomaniacal wish for terrible devastation," fulfilment of "a childish dream of revengeful omnipotence."

Jung, in his essay, "Answer to Job," struggles with the dilemma that the apocalyptic concept presents to man, both as a creature of faith and a vessel of contradictory drives. Jung in this piece of writing resembles Jacob wrestling with the Angel. He does not ask: if God made Atlantis into a Paradise on earth, why did he permit it to fall into evil habits, and why did he have the sea destroy it? But then, why did God permit Satan to torture Job—or, question of questions—did he allow Christ to die on the Cross? Love, Charity, Sin, Death, and Destruction; Jung sought to deal with all these themes. "What kind of father is it," he asked with engaging simplicity, "who would rather his son were slaughtered than forgive his ill-advised creatures who have been corrupted by his precious Satan?" Man, according to Jung, is "a vessel filled with divine conflict."

And that is precisely what our vision of Atlantis is today, in retrospect. Its rise and fall, its elusive reality and inescapable myth, dramatize the "divine conflict" within ourselves.

We now come to the final question: was Atlantis a rehearsal of our own eventual apocalyptic end? Mankind has a way of having its fears come true—perhaps because its unconscious fascination with disasters, like that of a child playing with matches, tends to bring about the very thing it dreads. Nuclear power has given us the means of doing to ourselves what the shuddering earth and the all-consuming sea did to Atlantean civilization. If the retrospective image of Atlantis we have today, a millennia-old event that has been magnified in the retelling, reflects our own duality—shouldn't we at least have a choice?

I began this book with a beguiling memory, a night spent in the rim of Mount Kintamani in Bali, the island that is the world's image of paradisical dreams. Within a few days of writing down these memories, news came that an earthquake just a few miles from Kintamani had wiped out the village of Seririt, killing at least 233 people and injuring more than 2,000. In midsummer of 1976, we were reminded that we cannot ever be complacent, that the real or imagined fate of Atlantis remains an ever-present threat.

We can now make our own eruptions. Since Hiroshima and Nagasaki, we need no Santorini or Krakatoa cataclysms to remind us of our precarious existence on the thin shell that is the earth's crust. The answer is simply that we must, we absolutely must, turn away from our fascination with destruction. Yet, we are what we are: Children yearning for the Lost Paradise, and still enthralled with the Ultimate Disaster that bears the name of Atlantis.

CHAPTER 17

Where Is the Real Atlantis?

The last evening I spent on Santorini, the center of today's Atlantis searches, a cordial group of visitors gathered at the local tavern. Our meal was just about finished. All of us who had come to the volcanic island for a variety of interests were in a joyful mood. I lifted a glass of a local white wine, naturally labeled "Atlantis," and proposed a simple toast: "To Plato, whose facts and ideas have brought us together here and now!"

It all started with Plato and his vague if dramatic description of an advanced but doomed Atlantis. There can be arguments about the actual period of such a civilization, about the details Plato reported, and about the size and population of the place—but that a highly developed society did exist, within the memory of Plato's ancestors and informants, and that it perished in a cataclysm, cannot be doubted.

We have examined some of the psychological reasons why the fate of Atlantis continues to fascinate us. Our generation has revived this interest dramatically; archaeological discoveries and underwater explorations have given scientific impetus to new hypotheses. Inevitably, each idea of when and where Atlantis existed is identified with the conclusions reached by a devoted and strong-minded personality. The steep donkey path that leads from the harbor to Thera, Santorini's major city atop the volcano's rim, is called "Spyridon Marinatos Street," in memory of the imaginative archaeologist who saw Santorini as the center of the cataclysm that destroyed Minoan civilization on Crete.

Today, at the Akrotiri site that has yielded delightful frescoes and other evidence of Minoan culture on Santorini, Marinatos' successor, Dr. Christos Doumas, continues the excavation project that has already given us unprecedented insights. Doumas has his own ideas on the role Santorini played in creating the Atlantis concept. He notes that "the form, dimensions, location and social life as set down by Plato do not accord with what archaeology has revealed" and adds that "Plato was using Atlantis as a philosophical device for conveying his ideas on the body politic and society."

Doumas believes the Atlantis legend has "some factual basis" in Santorini, as "the sinking of an island," and "the collapse of a civilization," the Minoan, which extended over a good deal of the Aegean Sea. Dr. Doumas politely disagrees with the hypothesis that Santorini (Thera) itself was Atlantis, complete with the advanced cultural features listed by Plato. Rather, Doumas notes, the Atlantis idea embraced "two separate occurrences due to the same causative factors," which by the passage of time were fused into "a single event." He feels that modern archaeological findings suggest that "the Egyptian priests who related the legend to Solon in the seventh century B.C. had recorded second hand information which was liable to be erroneous."

We can step back, in our own time, and view the emergence of the Atlantis legend without being dogmatically committed to a single hypothesis. Obviously, as the new science of underwater archaeology illustrates, we are the heirs to a variety of civilizations that sank without any records we have been able to find or decipher. Minoan script has not yielded texts that can be compared with the detailed information decoded from Babylonian tablets. Even the very word "Minoan" is only an inspired but artificial label: the British archaeologist, Sir Arthur Evans, who unearthed the Palace of Knossos on Crete, simply adapted the name of legendary King Minos and used it to name the civilization he discovered.

If Evans had called the advanced civilization he unearthed "Atlantoan" rather than "Minoan," many would by now take for granted that Atlantis had, indeed, been found. After all, what's in a name? The Atlantic Ocean, as we have seen, was named much later than Plato's Atlantis, although both have their linguistic root in the legendary strongman, Atlas. If Columbus had been given full credit for his discovery, the continent he encountered would have been named Columbia; instead, it became America, after Amerigo Vespucci, the Italian explorer of the Amazon region of South America.

One more example: Europe. In Greek mythology, Europa

was a Phoenician princess, whom Zeus, in the guise of a bull, took to Crete. The legendary King Minos was the result of their union. Now a whole continent is named after Europa, and most of us are totally unaware of this link between myth and geographical label. And of course, we're right back in Crete again, with King Minos and "Minoan civilization"—which, but for a whim of Arthur Evans, wasn't called "Atlantis."

When we stop and ask, at this point, "Where is the real Atlantis?" we are forced to reply: in the minds of men. Inspired by Plato, regions as different as Bimini in the Caribbean and the German island of Helgoland in the North Sea have been identified with the legendary sunken continent. One hypothesis, linked to the idea that Atlantis must have been located in the Atlantic Ocean, even concludes from the migration patterns of eels that these animals perform a semicircle around sections of the ocean, because they collectively "remember" Atlantis as an obstacle in millennia past. The ingenuity of such speculative thinking is admirable, although it need not be convincing.

Ignatius Donnelly's remarkable diligence as a researcher, powered by his intellectual restlessness and passion for detailed documentation, is responsible for many of the ideas we encounter even today. Egerton Sykes has told us that it was Donnelly's writings that first focused his attention on Atlantis; Sykes, in turn, brought together the ideas of other men, rangings from the earth's "capture" of the moon to the concept of "diffusion" of Atlantean civilization throughout the world.

Edgar Cayce popularized a combination of concepts: Atlantis and reincarnation. His "life readings" thrilled many who were told that they had lived through a series of earlier incarnations, often in ancient Egypt, Greece, and Rome—and of course, Atlantis. Who can fail to be intrigued by such a backward vision of his or her own identity? To have been a galley slave under the pharaohs, a daring soldier in ancient Sparta, and a scribe traveling with Roman legions in Gaul—after having been a priest on Atlantis—is surely enough to add retrospective glamour to the life of an insurance agent in Iowa. Under hypnosis, it is quite possible for an indivdual's memory to "regress" and add colorful detail from such earlier incarnations. Such memories or phantasies may have positive or negative results for a contemporary existence, ranging from reassurance to escapist delusion.

Wanda Sue Childress, who spent several years as a newspaper reporter in Los Angeles, says that California probably contains "the world's largest body of armchair Atlantisphiles." Southern California, specifically, has a concentration of students of the mystic arts, some of whom believe they have been re-born in California, together with other Atlanteans who were their brothers or sisters thousands of years ago.

Among these neo-Atlanteans, there is a popular belief that the United States is the "New Atlantis." They feel that the United States is giving mankind a "second chance"; it must avoid the pitfalls of the Atlanteans, who put power above spiritual development and were, therefore, doomed to extinction. These ideas are often linked with ambivalent feelings about a future cataclysmic fate, such as the often-prophesied earthquake that might result from a shift in the San Andreas Fault.

A small group of reincarnationists believe that the western portion of California is the last above-sea level vestige of that other legendary sunken continent, Lemuria, mentioned earlier in this volume. In California's occult pecking order, it makes a difference whether one has been reincarnated from Atlantis or Lemuria. Atlanteans are said to display an attitude of superiority, while Lemurians are more passive and less likely to engage in demonstrations of supernatural powers. Reincarnated Lemurians go about the business of being naturally psychic with an air of quiet confidence, while reincarnated Atlanteans tend to show off such achievements as reading minds, healing others, or engaging in prophetic utterances.

Scientific research into the facts behind the Atlantis idea, such as the underwater exploration of Jacques Cousteau in the Aegean, lends new credence to such related concepts as reincarnation and doomsday prophecy. The Atlanteans had their chance of spirtual development; they muffed it and were destroyed. We, according to these reincarnationists of the Atlantis persuasion, should make up for this failure in our past; but if we fail once more, cataclysm will overtake us, just as it did during the Atlantean incarnation.

When I said that the real Atlantis is in men's minds, I knew that what I wrote might sound like a smooth cop-out. It isn't! It is precisely the conclusion at which I have arrived after more than a quarter century of on-and-off fascination with the Atlantis legend, ranging from youthful enthrallment to mature and careful checking of the evidence. Speaking of Atlantis as the "once and future Paradise" in religio-psychological terms, places it, I believe, correctly within the area of basic human desire for a more perfect existence: the present has its share of fear and horror; let the past and future make up for the shortcomings we know all too well.

I see little wrong, and much to gain, by current efforts in the name of a search for Atlantis. Cousteau, as shrewd and knowledgeable a modern adventurer as can be imagined, is willing to utilize the Atlantis legend as a starting point for explorations into past civilizations. If people want to see his ventures in terms of Atlantis, well and good. The same, I feel, goes for other efforts, such as the Cayce-inspired Bimini explorations, efforts to find undersea structures off Western Europe's Atlantic coastline, and archaeological projects in other parts of the world.

The more we learn of our own past, the more we realize that knowledge comes in fragments that must be put together with skill and imagination—just as the Minoan frescoes from Crete and Santorini had to be assembled, bit by bit, into delightful mosaics. If we are truly objective, we must even look at Sir Arthur Evans' reconstruction of the Palace of Knossos on Crete and wonder whether it actually ever was as Evans told us. The British archaeologist has been criticized by other scholars, notably by Professor Hans G. Wunderlich, a geological authority from the German University at Stuttgart; he believes that the Knossos structure was, much like the pyramids, a temple for the dead, rather than a residence of the living. But his, too, is just another guess, despite geological clues and ingenious arguments. Even if Wunderlich were right, the beauties of Knossos reflect the delights of the living and an effort to have the dead enjoy them in an afterlife. But the findings on Santorini are definitely parts of living quarters, where we find the charms of Minoan civilization beyond any arguments concerning the realities and fate of Crete.

It all adds up to this: the Atlantis legend has spurred men of imagination into looking for traces of lost civilizations, and it has given them popular support in their otherwise specialized and esoteric tasks. If this has promoted people to look for Atlantis in geographic areas of which Plato could have had no knowledge, well and good; the magic name "Atlantis" inspires worthwhile searches that will enlighten us about our past, regardless of label. But those who believe that Plato's Atlantis was an extrapolation from one or a series of disasters in the Aegean connected with the Santorini volcano have geographic logic on their side.

Other islands may soon yield additional clues to the fate of Minoan civilization: beneath Homer's "wine-dark sea" lies a multitude of evidence. Right now, Dr. Doumas has extended his Santorini searches to the island of Rhodes, where the Trianda site promises additional evidence of Minoan civilization and its ultimate fate; other prospective targets are the site of Phylakopi on the island of Melos, and Saint Irene (Aghia Irini) on Kea.

But, back once more to Santorini. After the volcanic outbreak in the sixteenth century B.C., the island was deserted. Doumas writes in *Portrait of an Island: Santorini* that, according to Herodotus, it remained uninhabited until about 1330 B.C., five generations before the Trojan Wars. The Phoenicians came and stayed until about 1115 B.C., followed by the Dorians. Dr. Doumas adds: "After a Dark Age of almost two centuries, Thera emerged in the ninth century B.C. as a 'stepping stone' on the route from the south-east coast of the Greek mainland via Melos, Crete to Cyprus." After seven years of drought, in 630 B.C., the inhabitants of Thera left their barren island and settled on the North African coast. During Hellenistic times, Thera once again achieved prominence and was an active community; its importance faded during the centuries of the Roman Empire.

Today, the island of Santorini has become almost too accessible for its limited size and resources. One harbor, not deep enough for anchorage, has nevertheless been opened to make car and bus travel possible. In mid-1976, daily airline connections with Athens were established. The magic word "Atlantis" has made Santorini a tourist attraction. Slowly, donkeys are giving way to Mercedes buses.

Santorini is surely the center of the cataclysms that inspired the stories told by Egyptian priests to Solon, and recorded by Plato. In that sense, it is the center of all that Atlantis can mean to us today. It symbolizes—and archaeology above and below the sea documents it—the powerful pull which the concept of Atlantis has for our generation. We are in search of our unknown past, because we are in search of our own identity; we crave to understand our origins, as we live in awe of the past and fear of the future. Atlantis is more real than stones and murals; Atlantis is as real as our own hearts and minds.

APPENDIX A

On the Legend of Atlantis
by Spyridon Marinatos

Modern archaeological and marine geological research in the Aegean Sea of the Eastern Mediterranean is largely due to the vision and drive of one scholar, the late Dr. Spyridon Marinatos; his death in 1973 took place on the very site of his investigative work: the remnants in stone, shape, and art work that form today's research into the past on the island of Santorini (Thera). But the groundwork, at least in terms of hypotheses and concrete planning, was laid more than a quarter of a century earlier. It is vividly outlined by Dr. Marinatos himself in the following paper, a translation from the scholarly journal *Cretica Chronica*, Vol. IV, 1950.

Yet another contribution to over two thousand[1] books and publications which have been issued on the subject of Atlantis may perhaps seem in vain; from the purely scientific aspect it may even seem presumptuous. With these reservations in mind, Robert L. Scranton, known for his study on Greek fortifications and one of the latest Americans to do research on Atlantis, has added another page. In an article he proposed the very original if somewhat bold hypothesis that the legend of Atlantis was founded on the destruction of the big drainage works constructed by the Minyans resulting in the flooding of the plain of Orchomenos by the waters of Lake Copaïs.[2]

I also will attempt to expound on the subject with similar reservations but more so since even briefly informative bibli-

1. J. Trikkalinos, *Transactions of the Greek Anthropological Society,* 1948, p. 55. (In Greek)
2. R. Scranton, Lost Atlantis Found Again? *Archaeology*, 2, 3 (Autumn 1949), p. 159 f.

ography is not available to me.[3] This perhaps may not be a very important point because I intend to rely on an earlier theory for which I am the only responsible. This theory is related to the great eruption of Thera in approximately 1500 B.C. and which must undoubtedly have left a terrible imprint on the memories of the inhabitants of the Eastern Mediterranean of that time. Brief summaries of two lectures I gave on the subject in Athens were published in the *Transactions of the Anthropological Society of Athens* (1948, pp. 50-55).

An examination of the subject from the geological aspect would, I believe, serve no useful purpose and would indeed be beyond my province so I will simply quote my colleague in that field Prof. J. Trikkalinos, who writes: " ... no evidence can be adduced to justify the hypothesis of an extensive area of land in the Atlantic, i.e. Atlantis, which could subsequently have disappeared during historical times."

I propose herein to examine the problem of the legend of Atlantis in greater detail and this may well lead to more concrete conclusions. We must first resolve whether we are confronted with fable or historical legend. If it is the latter, the typical form through which all myths containing an historical core are transmitted must be studied and then, wherever possible, we must try to detach the purely historical elements and combine them with one another in order to reach a more or less historical conclusion.

I think we may safely preclude the fable. Plato's imagination could not possibly have conjured up an account so unique and unusual to classical literature—it was only later that this form of writing appears, such as Lucian employs in his "True History"—nor does the account follow this form. For this reason the account is usually called a "tradition" by Plato. I should also like to add that if in some parts the account chances to bear the stamp of the fable this must be attributed to the Egyptians and not to Plato. In fact, we possess a story from the time of the Middle Kingdom (2000-1750 B.C. approximately) preserved on papyrus and now to be found in Leningrad. This is the famous "tale of the shipwrecked traveler" wherein an Egyptian relates how he was shipwrecked whilst sailing to Pharaoh's mines—presumably to Sina. His prudent precautions proved unavailing although he had

3. I know only by name the last or one of the last books on the subject (Georges Poisson, *L'Atlantide devant la science*, Paris 1945).

selected a ship 120 cubits long and 40 cubits wide, in which "were the finest Egyptian sailors. They knew the sky, they knew the earth and their heart was stauncher than a lion's. They could foretell the tempest before it burst and bad weather before it broke". Notwithstanding, a dreadful storm blew up and a wave 8 cubits high, born by the wind, shattered the ship and all were lost save our shipwrecked traveler who, clinging to a log, was cast up on an island. There, a wonderful dragon lived which was 30 cubits long and whose body was encased in gold; its beard, which was more than 2 cubits long and its eyebrows were of pure lapis lazuli. It snatched up the shipwrecked man in its jaws and bore him to its lair. However, it did him no harm and on hearing his tale informed him that he was "on an island of the sea and both its shores lie in the midst of the waves . . . This is an island of blissful beings where all the heart may desire can be found and its riches abound. . . ." It continued by telling him that its brothers with their children, in all 75 sublimely happy dragons, lived on the island but that once, when it was absent, a star fell which burnt them all up to a cinder. It then went on to prophesy that very shortly the Egyptian would be taken away by a ship belonging to his countrymen and that he would die happy with his family around him. It heaped him with gifts and revealed that it was the sovereign of Punt and that all perfumes and myrrh belonged to it. But, it added, "never more shall you see this island because it will be swallowed up by the waves."[4] This tale of a supremely happy island with its contented people which later became submerged and vanished was, therefore, clearly familiar to the Egyptians. This is the tale the Saite priest confused with other traditional accounts concerning Atlantis because they contained similarities. We must now examine the manner in which historical legends are handed down to the people from mouth to mouth.

The instincts of a people's soul are identical in all ages and civilizations, perhaps this is why the historical legends of all nations are delivered in a typical manner usually possessing the following elements: Names become transformed or corrupt. Events actually having occurred are intermixed with

4. Published by Golenischeff, *Les papyrus hiératiques de l'érmitage impérial de St. Petersburg*, 1913, and *Le Conte du Naufragé*, Cairo, 1912. Erman-Ranke, Aegypten 603-605.

imaginary acounts. The districts where the events took place are changed to others and, moreover, time is projected indefinitely back into the past. Various ages and personalities are fused into a single period and into a single figure. Some of the names are usually preserved and quite often, some of the cultural achievements which, however, are interwoven with the fabric of the story. Tradition is diversified by insignificant events of the kind that appeal to the popular imagination whereas events that may possess a capital historical significance are passed over. Examples of this type, belonging to a later date, are the traditions related to Alexander the Great and Attila the Hun—wherein Edgel becomes Nibel and, in Scandinavia, Atli.

Eduard Meyer, the famous historian, does not allow this point to pass unobserved and notes:[5]

Historical events are introduced into popular mythological cycles ... they are mixed with material of other provenance, partly from myths partly from stories, and are thus subjected to radical change. The Trojan war is incorporated in the myth of Helen and of Achilles afterwards constantly expanding—the myth of Odysseus. The myth of the Seven of Thebes appears in conjunction with the myth of Oedipus and Teiresias and this, furthermore, is associated with the myth related to Amphiaraus, a god of neighboring Oropos in the country of the Graeans. These traditions, originally independent, later became part of the myth of war against Thebes ... hence the myth of the duel between two brothers—Eteocles is the king of neighboring Orchomenos but the name Polyneikes is a fabrication—which is a very widely disseminated popular theme. The historical kernel is clear nevertheless. This famous scholar on pre-history and on history goes on further: We need not imagine that the war of the Seven was a world-shattering event; heroic myths of other peoples, especially those of the Germans, point to the fact that insignificant events—e.g., the overthrow of the Burgundian state of Worms—are often given pride of place in the myths whereas events of far greater importance, such as the Roman invasion, have virtually left no trace on the memory of the people ... The overthrow of the Thebes of Cadmus by the Boeotians during the "Völkerwanderung" of the peoples is wrongly attributed to

5. Eduard Meyer, *Geschichte des Altertums* 2, 1 (2nd edition, 1928), pp. 256-8.

the remote period. Eduard Meyer refers here to the well-known fact that the epic of the Nibelungen is related to the events in Burgundy. An analogous example, taken from the Sumerian civilization, would be the rivalry between two impoverished dynasties, those of Larsa and Isin whose fall so vividly impressed the popular imagination that it even marked a starting point for dating, whereas far more important events such as the exploits of Eannatum, or the great Lugal Zaggizi and even Sargon the Great of Agad, left no equally marked imprint.

An outstanding and typical example of this form of events, as outlined above, is provided by Herodotus whose sources of information were nearly always derived from the people and from popular narratives as well as from the ubiquitous lay guides who were even then, as are their modern counterparts, a plague. The people believed that the most memorable works and achievements in Babylon belonged to two queens, Semiramis and Nitocris and especially to the latter; this was told to Herodotus. And yet no queen ruled over Babylon. Semiramis was indeed a figure in history but merely as queen mother of Assyria and never as queen, being at most the Trustee for four years of her son Adad Nirari IV during his minority about 810 B.C. As for Nitocris, to whom were attributed the works of a number of kings, as for example Nebuchadnezzar II, she never existed. Again nearly all the achievements of a whole host of famous Egyptian rulers were attributed by the people to a single king, Sesostris. He was a historical figure and a great king of the 12th Dynasty (1900 B.C.); events covering whole centuries were, however, attributed to him alone because only his name was ready to the tongue of the people. As Spiegelberg the Egyptologist has observed, it was from such sources that Herodotus drew his information. He also explains how when Herodotus visited the pyramids his lay guides told him a story about fantastic quantities of garlic and onions consumed by the workmen who built them.[6]

6. Herodotus 2, 125 (sixteen hundred talents of silver were supposed to have been spent on these delicacies during the construction of the pyramid of Cheops). See W. Spiegelberg, Die Glaubwürdigkeit von Herodots Bericht über Aegypten im Lichte der aegyptischen Denkmäler (Orient und Antike 3) p. 16, note 12. Herodotus visited Egypt for 3½ months from August to November in about 450. There may be two autographs by him because two sherds bearing

Confining ourselves to a single example from Greece, perhaps one of the most illuminating, we have a similar case in the historical myths about Minos. Today we know that there were many palaces in Crete, each with a life span between five and seven centuries. Many glorious men must have breathed their spirit into those palaces and have made them famous through the medium of their brilliant personalities. Yet practically all the recollections of the men of antiquity concerning Crete are centered on one sole dynast, Minos of Knossos, whom they sometimes duplicated—Minos the older or the first and Minos the younger or the second—because they could see that it was impossible to ascribe to a single person all the events that were commemorated.[7]

We shall now proceed to examine the myth about Atlantis. Since we are faced not only with the problem of locality—the Atlantic Ocean—but with the apparently greater one mentioned in the narrative, that of time—the events connected with Atlantis supposedly occurred nine thousand years before the narrative—we must say a few words on this colossal anachronism.

Nowadays we are able to follow with certainty the great civilizations of our planet to 4000 B.C., that is to say a period of six thousand years before the present day. Evidence of man, so the specialists tell us, may be followed for 600,000 years and possibly for one million years; the history of the evidence of life for up to 800,000,000 years. All this knowledge has impressed man's thinking. The oldest European nations do not number more than one thousand years of continuous political history and life; the oldest of the historical nations of Europe, Greece, not more than three thousand to three thousand five hundred, the Egyptians and the Sumerians about five thousand. The Middle Age was content to date the beginning of the world, according to the traditions of Israel at the year 4004 B.C. which simply coincides with the

his name written in a form of script belonging to the middle of the 5th century B.C. were found within the sacred precinct (Hellenium) in Naucratis, where visitors used to dedicate vases, *op. cit.*, p. 13. Popular belief attributed to Sesostris works and conquests of Pharaohs who lived 700 years later (Thotmes III Amenophis or Amenhotep III and especially to Rameses II), *op. cit.* p. 24.

7. My paper on the royal genealogies of Crete, in the forthcoming *Mélanges Charles Picard*, will deal with this more fully.

dark beginning of the two great civilizations mentioned above.[8]

Ever since then progress has been steady and spectacular. Man discovered new continents. He then circumnavigated the earth. Then, in spite of the objections of the church and the superstition and dangers which the Galilei of science had to overcome, telescopes and spectroscopes probed the chaos of the Universe. Today we are able to measure more precisely how minute a fraction of matter is the Earth within the Universe and how slight a moment in time in the life of the Earth is taken up by the history of human civilization. How far back then do the memories of man reach? This is of paramount importance to the problem of Atlantis. Millions of years were necessary for the earth to cool to the restricted and low lying land and the immense oceans of the Paleozoic period. Algae, coral, molluscs and similarly primitive specimens of life appeared on our planet. Trees, forests and new forms of life, especially the giant saurians, developed during the Mesozoic period. The Tertiary period saw great alterations to the crust of the planet. The former beasts disappeared and enormous mammals took their place, animals now extinct which disappeared during the course of the period. Towards the end of the same period the most advanced example of pithecanthropus appeared, from which man later was torn off from the original family of the primates and developed separately. All these evolutions are calculated in terms of millions of years.

The last period, the Quaternary to which we belong, is divided into two sections: the earlier and the later. The earlier possessed an animal life that became extinct—mammoths, the Elephas antiquus, cave bears and deer. Glaciers spread and contracted in turn.

The last geological formations that shaped the continents into their present form are bound with this period. For example, before the beginning of this period, the later Quaternary, approximately 20,000 years B.C., England became detached from the European continent, Africa became finally separated from Europe and the Mediterranean was formed once the links that untied the two continents by the extension of Spain

8. See Arnold Toynbee, the British historian in his *Civilization on Trial* (1948) p. 151-2, in which he expresses similar and more advanced views in his well-known original style.

and Italy had ceased to exist. At about this period also, the Aegeis became submerged as well as the land that spanned Europe and North America; perhaps also the land that united East Asia with Alaska.

Having made this digression we may well ask whether it was possible for primitive man of that period to have been able to retain memories of these geological phenomena. It is assumed that man may have passed, in primitive times, through Sunda towards Australia before the formation of Polynesia in the straights of Sunda as we know it today. Waves of tribes may likewise have passed towards America through the Alaskan corridors as well as men and animals from Europe to Asia through the above mentioned corridors of the Mediterranean; of these movements no recollection has been preserved.

Man's oldest geological recollections are those about the Flood. We know of many floods due to storm water or to tidal waves and they are remembered in all the continents except perhaps that of Africa. This particular flood, that of the Bible (the Greeks had other traditions of their own concerning floods) dates back to the time of ancient civilizations and to that of the Sumerians. This was the source of the Hebrew tradition. The excavations at Ur show that a disaster actually occurred around 4000 B.C. Therefore, since the version told in Egypt states that Atlantis lay beyond the Pillars of Hercules, that is the Atlantic Ocean of today, and that nine thousand years had elapsed between the sinking of Atlantis and the time of the discussion between Solon and the Saite priests, it follows that we are dealing with impossibilities. Even in the case of England becoming detached or of dry land being submerged in the West Atlantic—the Sargasso Sea, if this is at all thinkable—or an event that actually occurred according to geological data, it would be impossible for man to retain recollections of events so far removed in time.

Therefore we can only accept the historical core of the traditions on Atlantis as a fact, as it happens in other historical traditions, but time and place we cannot accept. There is also evidence that the chronology in the hands of the Egyptians and the Sumerians, was exaggerated beyond all reason. There is one positive fact noted by tradition which will immediately guide us to the correct chronological framework, the flowering "Hellas" which is an undeniable element in the story of

Atlantis. This inevitably brings us to the 16th-15th century B.C. when the Creto-Mycenaean civilization was at its peak. Now we are ready to examine in detail the account of the Atlantis as follows.

Critias[9] tells us about a very important tradition concerning the greatness of Athens. The source of this tradition is Solon who told it to Dropides, Critias's great grandfather with whom the great law-giver had strong family ties. Then Critias's grandfather, also called Critias, repeated it in front of his grandson. This, briefly, is what he heard: Solon,[10] during his visit to Egypt, spoke with the priests of Neith ("Athene") in Sais. In the course of the conversation, Solon took the opportunity to tell the Egyptians, whose past was incomparable and of which they were very proud, all he knew about Greece that was most ancient. He spoke therefore about Phoroneus and Niobe and about the Deucalion flood, whereupon one of the priests said:

Solon, Solon, you Greeks are never anything but children, for you know of nothing that is ancient. Firstly, you speak of a cataclysm whereas many have occurred. Other disasters were also brought about by fire when changes in the order of the universe occur. When you speak of Phaethon you are referring to this fact. After each disaster the cultured and educated elements of the population were destroyed and only the shepherds on the mountains remained. This is why you remember nothing. Nine thousand years ago, however, you accomplished a magnificent deed because you then humbled a mighty and arrogant power that had come from the Atlantic sea where there was an island larger than Asia and Africa together over which ruled a glorious line of kings who, at one time, extended their domination as far as Tyrrhenia and the Egyptian borders. There came a day when they attempted to overcome both you and us in a single campaign. Then you placed yourselves at the head and stood firm; you did not relinquish the struggle even though your allies abandoned you in the field. You faced death but finally you were victorious and thus prevented our subjection and freed those who had been enslaved. Afterwards, earthquakes and cataclysms oc-

9. Plato, Timaeus 21b f.
10. Solon lived from 640/39 to 559/8 B.C. He emigrated to Egypt some time after 572. He was away for 10 years during which he visited other countries.

curred; within one day and one terrible night, your army was engulfed by the earth and Atlantis likewise, submerged by the sea, disappeared. This is the reason why the open sea is not navigable there and is unexplored on account of the quantities of mud left on the sea bed by the submerged island.[11]

The narrative, varied with theories on cosmogony and philosophy, is long.[12] Our knowledge of Egyptian literature and thought is today sufficiently advanced to allow us to distinguish between the purely Egyptian elements of the account and the evidence of Plato's Greek intellect. This is not essential here and the summary is enough for our purpose.

We may thus observe that the legend as it stands cannot be accepted. We can however separate fantasy from fact which, as long as the problem of place and especially that of time are solved, is quite clear and easily identifiable according to the principles of the origin of historical legends, as we have exposed above. The explanations of where the submerged island lay will be discussed below. As for the chronology of nine thousand years, we now know that no Greeks existed then to perform heroic deeds nor Egyptians to write them down. The so-called Pyramid texts, the oldest continuous texts of the Egyptians, belong to about the middle of the third millennium but concern religious formulas only. We possess historical texts of substantial length only after the

11. This last feature attracted some scholars to search for Atlantis in the Sargasso Sea near the Antilles where quantities of weed by the same name floating in the sea are a nuisance to shipping. I personally believe such a reminiscence to be likely because we are apt to underestimate the daring feats of ancient seafarers (See below for the circumnavigation of Africa by the Phoenicians). For that matter, Plato's narrative could (Timaeus 24ᵉ - 25ᵉ) be considered as the first reference to the existence of America. After Atlantis has been described as lying beyond Gibraltar, then the narrative continues that from here one could sail to other islands, and indeed to *the* other islands (therefore they must have been very well known) and from there "opposite to all continent surroundings that veritable sea". Did not Columbus (the third to do so, since he was preceded by the Vikings) rediscover America in the same way? He first put in at S. Salvador, one of the Bahamas: then, he was informed, there was a great continent to the West, later to be known as America.
12. Thus, for instance, the theory about the world being destroyed by floods or by fire (Timaeus 22 c) is that of the Babylonians about fire and flood, later to be adopted by the Stoics. See B. Meisner, *Babylonian und Assyrien* II, 118.

18th dynasty. The most considerable are those belonging to the time of Thotmes III (1500-1447) and those of Ramesses II (1292-1225), and the later texts of Merenptah and Ramesses III. I consider these last as being the texts that the Saite priest had in mind whilst conversing with Solon.

In another dialogue[13] according to Plato, the Egyptians in discussing the war against the Atlantians repeatedly referred to Cecrops, Erechtheus, Erysichthon and others who lived before Theseus. Plato, it is true, asserts that those same names were given in succession. Any way, the events taken as a whole testify, apart from Plato's opinions, that we are within the framework of the second millennium, the only possible one. The simplest method would, I believe, be to sketch an outline of the history of Egypt parallel to that of the Creto-Mycenaean area during the second millennium to be followed by some words on the years of the Saite period. Thus the matter, as regards the elements from which the legend of Atlantis was woven, will speak for itself. The period between the Middle and New Kingdom, exactly 200 years (1780-1580) is occupied nearly entirely by the domination of the Hyksos (according to Manetho these were "shepherds") kings who were foreign occupants of the throne and of semitic origin. The revolt against them was organized by the local princes of Thebes. Today nearly all scholars are agreed that this was done with outside help and that the expelling of the Hyksos was achieved with the help of considerable forces other than Egyptian. This fact, moreover, is to be found mentioned in Egyptian sources which refer to those who went to their help under the general name of Hannebt or Hanebu. Unfortunately this word does not always have the same meaning because sometimes it is used for the inhabitants of the Libyan coast (especially earlier) and at others for those of the islands of the Aegean Sea. The famous Eduard Meyer unhesitatingly accepts the latter. The revered Queen Mother Aahhotep bears the title "Princess of the coast of Hanebu" and from this title, which we shall never encounter again

13. Critias 110 a-b. We have no way of knowing, of course, whether the narrative is genuinely Egyptian or invented by Plato, which is, surely, more likely. However, the Egyptians may have memorized some of the names of the great Mycenaean tradition. It is, however, not important because we know that if the Egyptians had noted any events of the "remote" Aegean age, those events could not possibly have been attributed to other than the 2nd millennium.

through all centuries of Egyptian literature, he concludes that she was married to a Cretan prince. The Hyksos were, therefore, beaten with the help of the Cretans.[14]

Apart from this theory, which is indeed not acceptable to other historians, I hope to publish shortly a study proving that the Mycenaeans and not the unwarlike Cretans went to the help of the Egyptians. The Cretans must certainly have contributed by transporting the Mycenaean warriors in their ships. I believe that the great quantity of gold discovered by Schliemann in the royal cemetery of the acropolis was certainly the price for their assistance to the Egyptians. Those stout but simple warriors brought new burial customs from Egypt, the mummies, face masks, funeral stelae and the rich funeral furnishings. A better explanation for the sudden "miracle" of the Mycenaeans in the midst of the poor and frugal Middle Helladic period, cannot be found.

The mercenaries from the Aegean area never since then ceased to assist the Egyptians. At first it was thought that the "Shardana" were the mercenaries of Egypt only during the period of Ramesses II, but the Amarna tablets have proved that they had been employed earlier than this for the garrisons of Syria. Therefore the conclusions that Meyer draws are that their use dating from the beginning of the New Kingdom[15] is very probable. The best proof is the constant intercourse between the two areas, the Egyptian and the Creto-Mycenaean, from the 16th century and onwards. An entire book has been devoted to Egyptian finds in Greece (J. Pendlebury, *Aegyptiaca*).

The peoples of the Mediterranean did not always visit Egypt as friends. Either on looting expeditions or under pressure from the waves of the great migrations of the peoples of the 13th and 12th centuries, armed groups of various Mediterranean races invaded Egypt. Merenptah and Ramesses III fought hard and successfully to repulse them. Egypt was still sufficiently powerful to withstand these invaders amongst which we find the Akaiwasha, Danuna, Tursha, Shekelesh and Shardana who are identified with the Achaeans, Danaans, Tyrrhenians, Sicilians and Sardinians. The Pulesatim or Pelestim are usually identified with the Philistines and, more rarely, with the Pelasgians.

14. Ed. Meyer, *Gesch. d. Altertums*, 2, 1, p. 54-55.
15. Ed. Meyer, *op. cit.* 57.

After the 20th dynasty Egypt virtually enters the period of its decline. Weak and divided and its end preordained (the fate of all peoples who rely on mercenaries), it fell a prey to the Assyrians. Its last blaze of glory was the 26th dynasty of the period known as the Saite (663-525). The role of the Greeks was then of great significance as regards our subject. Psammetich I shook off the foreign yoke, as it was one thousand years previously, with the aid of Carian and mainly Ionian mercenaries. He conquered Syria and fought against the Scythians. Necho his son (609-593), the victor of the Asians, relied once more on the Greeks. We could say that the Ionians were his gods. After each victory, the great pharaohs of the new Kingdom offered up magnificent gifts to the god Ammon of Thebes. These consisted of gold and other metals, new buildings, animals and even slaves. Amasis, however, did not offer his gifts to Ammon on Thebes but to Apollo of the Branchidae and perhaps the most interesting point is that the offering was a truly simple one, but very Greek, it was the king's own panoply. One looks in vain for a similar case in the preceding history of Egypt. Greek ideas now penetrated Egypt. For the first time in the history of this proud and ancient country permission is given to build an Ionian colony, Naucratis, which became the earliest center of Hellenism in Egypt. The pharaohs now became imbued with the new culture and the new ideas of the Greeks in spite of the traditional conservatism of the Egyptian race, as Breasted has aptly observed. Necho attempted to open the Suez Canal to the Red Sea and sent Phoenician sailors to explore Africa. The sailors returned after an absence of three years and were the first to circumnavigate the African continent more than two thousand years before Vasco da Gama.

Psammetich II (593-588) the son of Necho, led his Greek mercenaries to Abu Simbel in Nubia where on the leg of the colossal statue of Ramesses II they carved their inscriptions. Apries and Amasis who followed are well-known figures to us from Greek sources and also from the friendship between Amasis and Polycrates the tyrant of Samos. In 525 the conquest of Egypt of Cambyses cut short the thread of the age long independence of the Egyptians.[16]

16. Special references are, in my opinion, unnecessary. The works of Ed. Meyer and especially James H. Breasted's, *A History of Egypt*, are sufficient.

The corresponding sketch of the Creto-Mycenaean history is simpler. A steady flow of intercourse between Crete and Egypt is evidenced as far back as the 12th dynasty and the name of Kyan, the Hyksos pharaoh, was found carved on the lid of an alabaster pyxis found in Knossos. After 1600 B.C. Mycenae entered the scene as an international power. At the time of Hatsepsout and Thotmes III, i.e., about 1500 or a little earlier, the Keftiu are often portrayed on the graves of the necropolis of Thebes bearing gifts. The Keftiu may possibly have been Cretans or equally well they may not. Many of the gifts, however, are incontestably of Creto-Mycenaean origin. The decorative motifs of the art of the two regions so influenced one another that it is often difficult to decide who lent what to whom.

A terrible disaster struck Crete in about 1500 B.C. Cities, monumental structures and two of the three palaces were destroyed for all time. Even the sacred caves such as that of Arcalochori collapsed. This disaster, for which the Achaeans could not possibly have been responsible,—since it occurred before their time—I have attributed to a tremendous natural event, the eruption of Thera. Of this theory we shall say only what is essential to our purpose.[17]

Thera, like all volcanic islands, was originally almost round and covered with vegetation—olive trees, palm trees—and flourishing settlements, as the volcano had for long been inactive. When the volcano erupted, pumice and ashes entirely covered the settlements. We know from the finds that the eruption must have occurred in about 1500. We are able to study the course and results of this eruption from later eruptions of the same volcano and from the eruption of the sister volcano Kracatoa—between Java and Sumatra—in 1883. Philippson tells us that what occurred in Kracatoa must have been identical with what occurred in Thera because both volcanoes belong to the same family. During the eruption or series of eruptions of Kracatoa, which lasted for three days, the following phenomena were observed. The ejected volcanic ash reached the stratosphere and for six months it floated on the atmosphere carried by the winds as far as Europe. (The splendid sunsets of that year were attributed to this.) Day turned to night over a radius of 150 kilometers and over the same area walls cracked and all swinging objects were subject-

17. I published a more detailed report in *Antiquity*, 1939, p. 425-439.

ed to continuous and terrifying motion. This and the clashing of mobile articles wrought indescribable agitation on men and animals which even though driven away by force would not leave the rooms. The terrible noise could be heard 3.500 kilometers away, in Australia, and, according to some, as far as the Antipodes. Be that as it may, this was the greatest historically verified noise on this planet. The volcano emitted colossal volumes of lava which not only covered the island but also the surrounding sea and even a harbor of neighboring Sumatra was blocked for a long time. A series of tidal waves 15 meters high struck the neighboring islands and caused the greatest havoc. Rocks became displaced, railway lines and locomotives were uprooted or overturned, and towns such as Telong-Betoeng in neighboring Sumatra, were literally wiped away. The steamship *Maruw,* suspended by a wave over the town, was later found several kilometers away in a forest. Any house that escaped the waves was destroyed by fire caused by lamps overturning. Thunderbolts met in the atmosphere charged with static electricity, striking lighthouses and tall buildings. Thirty-seven thousand souls were lost during this terrible disaster.

The area which exploded and sank in Thera is 80 square kilometers, that of Kracatoa some 20 square kilometers. The eruption must therefore have been "four" times as violent. The layer of ash covering the eastern part of the island that survived is today 30-60 meters thick. We know from later small eruptions that pumice covered the sea as far as the shores of Asia Minor. Since the speed of the waves is in ratio to the depth of the sea, which in the instance of the sea between Thera and Crete reaches a depth ten times and, in places, thirty times that of the sea at Kracatoa, the waves must have been more fearful and have traveled much faster. The fact that the waves then reached Crete—a distance of 60 miles—in a very short space of time is mathematically certain; there they caused enormous havoc on the low-lying land.

According to the late Professor N. Criticos, a typical phenomenon in the eruptions of Thera is the series of earthquakes extending over a widespread area around the Eastern Mediterranean proceding or following the eruptions of the volcano. There can be no doubt that Crete became deserted. The tradition that it was deserted was never forgotten by the inhabitants because Herodotus mentions and attributes it to Praisian—Eteocretan—tradition although he connects it to other times and other causes. The phenomena related to the eruption of Kracatoa can no longer leave us in doubt that here the eruption must have been far more intense and also that it must have been felt in Egypt. It is indeed curious that no relative evidence has so far been discovered.[18]

Crete steadily declined since then. The temporary prolongation of the life of the palace of Knossos alone by 50-100 years was not sufficient to stem the flow of events. In 1500, Peloponnesos, with Mycenae at its head, took the place of Crete. Amenhotep III, the most magnificent of all Egyptian kings (1411-1375 approximately), maintained close ties with Mycenae and no longer with Crete.

Yet, about a century later, in the region of the Mycenaean civilization, replete with riches, glory, warlike atmosphere and most vital international relations we feel more and more the Mycenaean rulers concerned with the first signs of danger. The Mycenaean acropolises were strengthened. Mycenae and Tiryns built supplementary walls and the great acropolis of Gla was hurriedly built. There was no time to build even a proper palace within its walls. Disaster was obviously imminent and between 1200 and 1100 all the centers of Mycenaean civilization were finally destroyed.

The elements of the historical legend of Atlantis may readily be placed now within this historical setting. In an article in the *Times* of London (19 January 1909) someone already had ventured to write anonymously subsequent to the splendid discoveries made in the Cretan soil, in which he maintained that this was the "Atlantis" of the Egyptians. He stressed the similarities between the tradition concerning Atlantis and the finds in Crete (capture of bulls without the use of weapons, organization, laws, etc.) and the flourishing intercourse between the island and Egypt (Keftiu, etc.). Then with the sudden disappearance of the Cretans (the author had no explanation for this) with the domination of the Mycenaeans, the Egyptians invented the myth of an island that became submerged. This article received some notice; others hastened to support the same views whereupon the author

18. Herodotus, 7, 11.

was encouraged to return, this time in a scientific journal and to sign himself: this was K. Frost.[19]

I believe this to be the most reasonable explanation. A large, prosperous and powerful island lost within the region of Egyptian awareness other than Crete did not exist. But that they should have invented a myth about its being submerged, even though they had their own story of the Shipwrecked Traveler, seems difficult. We then have the army of the Athenians which the "earth engulfed" to a man after frightful earthquakes and deluges within a single day and night,[20] together with Atlantis. The Egyptians must undoubtedly have learnt of an island becoming submerged and this was Thera, but being so small and insignificant they did not know of it. They transferred this event to Crete, the island so grievously struck and with which all contact they suddenly lost. The myth of an army being engulfed stemmed from the news of the loss of thousands of souls. With the lack of cohesion and logic that characterizes myths—as well as all other products of the peoples' imagination—not even Plato sensed the inconsistency of Atlantis in the Atlantic Ocean and the entire armed forces of the Athenians, in Athens of course, being submerged at one and the same time!

Why is the army that of the Athenians and the achievements again theirs? The explanation once more, is simple: the Saite priest was speaking to Solon the Athenian. The Athenians were Ionians. The Saite knew that for generations Egypt had relied on Ionian foot soldiers (hoplites) and had acquired her independence in the reign of Psammetich I with their help. The Ionians, therefore, are the bravest of all soldiers. Hence the exploit against the Atlantians!

The tradition of the domination of the Atlantians as far as Libya and Tyrrhenia and the threat to the Greeks and Egyptians whose land in the Delta they attempted to seize,[21] is equally clear. We know indeed that sea-faring peoples attacked Egypt through the Delta and were partially crushed in naval battles, as the reliefs of Ramesses III at Medinet Habu testify.[22] The fortifications of the Mycenaean acropolises, as

19. The Critias and Minoan Crete, JHS 33, 189 f.
20. Plato's Timaeus, 25 c-d.
21. Timaeus, 25 b.
22. See Ed. Meyer, Gesch. des Altertums 2, 1, Pl. VI. Bossert, Altkreta 3, fig. 552.

we have already said, obviously point to danger. It is reasonable to believe that amidst the wild surge of migrations during the 13th century B.C. we may justly accept that wandering peoples attacked or attempted to attack Greece before they reached Egypt. If this indeed happened they were most certainly repulsed because we possess no evidence of wholesale destruction of the Mycenaean civilization during that period.[23] They reached Egypt exhausted. Hence the tradition of the Egyptians that "the Athenians saved the Egyptians by overwhelming the Atlantians." We know so little about the history of the area covered by the Mycenaean civilization that this tradition may well be true. Some very large army from the westernmost Mediterranean countries—Tursa, Shekelesh and Shardana—may well have been destroyed by the mighty dynasts of the Mycenaean civilization.

An explanation for the transfer of the site of the island submerged in the Atlantic Ocean remains to be given. Two events will assist us; first, the then recent circumnavigation of Africa during the reign of Necho. The returning sailors must have recounted wonderful tales such as all sailors love to invent. On the other hand, the Saite priests I believe knew of peoples who had at some time started from the confines of the Mediterranean to attack Egypt, from the reliefs at Medinet Habu and from other sources. These then were the "Atlantian warriors."

Thus the myth about Atlantis may be considered as historical tradition which, in the manner typical of the distortion of such events, grew from the fusion of various disparate episodes. The destruction of Thera accompanied by terrible natural phenomena, felt as far away as Egypt, and the simultaneous disappearance of the Cretans from the trade with Egypt, gave rise to a myth of an island, beyond all measure powerful and rich, being submerged. The transference of the

23. [Note of 1969.] Now it is rather clear that the Mycenaean civilization persisted indeed for some time in Greece. But, on the other side, the palaces were burned and plundered and many Mycenaeans had to retreat to the islands or to remote districts of the country after Myc. III b, around 1250 B.C. This seems to be the result of a furious and plundering and catastrophic, but temporary invasion. There are many historical parallels of such later invasions of barbarians, devastating and flying like a typhoon. (Latest book: V. R. d' A. Desborough, The Last Mycenaeans and their Successors, Oxford 1964).

island to the Atlantic Ocean is explained by the circumnavigation of Africa by the Phoenician sailors. Invasions by central Mediterranean peoples were added to the myth as invaders from Atlantis. Their repulse by the Mycenaeans in conjunction with the bravery of the Ionian hoplites in the service of the Saite kings, were the elements from which stemmed the myth of an invincible Athenian army. The core of these events, embodied in a single historical myth, is the eruption of Thera and the year is about 1500 B.C. The most recent elements of the myth descend to about 600 B.C. Nine hundred years have thus been covered which the Saite priest projected tenfold into the abyss of the past. It thus reached, together with so much else that was impossible, the impossible chronology of nine thousand years before Solon's era.

BIBLIOGRAPHY

Berlitz, Charles, *The Mystery of Atlantis*. New York: Grosset & Dunlap, 1969.

Boettcher, Alfred (Ed.), *Portrait of an Island: Santorini*. Aachen: Mayer'sche Buchhandlung, 1974.

Bowman, John S., *Guide to Santorini*. Athens: Efstathidis Bros., 1974.

Cayce, Edgar Evans, *Edgar Cayce on Atlantis*, New York: Warner Paperback Library, 1968.

Corliss, William, *Mysteries Beneath the Sea*. New York: Crowell, 1970.

Donnelly, Ignatius, *Atlantis: The Antediluvian World*, revised and edited by Egerton Sykes. New York: Harper & Row, 1949.

Evans, Sir Arthur, *The Palace of Minos*. London: Macmillan, 1921.

Ferro, Robert, and Grumley, Michael, *Atlantis: The Autobiography of a Search*. New York: Doubleday, 1970.

Luce, J. V., *The End of Atlantis*. London: Thames & Hudson, 1969.

Ludwig, Emil, *Schliemann: The Story of a Gold-Seeker*. Boston: Little, Brown, 1931.

Marinatos, Spyridon, *Excavations at Thera* (Vols. I to VII). Athens: Library of the Athenian Archaeological Society, 1968-1976.

Mavor, James W., Jr., *Voyage to Atlantis*. New York: G. P. Putnam's, 1969.

Meyer, Ernst, *Heinrich Schliemann: Kaufmann und Forscher*. Göttingen: Musterschmidt-Verlag, 1969.

Muck, Otto, *Alles über Atlantis*. Düsseldorf: Econ-Verlag, 1976.

Ninkovich, D., and Heezen, B. C., "The Santorini Tephra," in *Submarine Geology and Physics*. Bristol: Colston Research Society, 1965.

Page, D. L., *The Santorini Volcano and the Destruction of Minoan Greece*. London: Society for the Promotion of Hellenic Studies, 1970.´

Perry, Richard, *The Unknown Ocean*, New York: Taplinger, 1972.

Pool, Lynn and Gray, *One Passion, Two Loves: The Story of Heinrich and Sophia Schliemann, Discoverers of Troy*. New York: T.Y. Crowell, 1966.

Schliemann, Heinrich. *Selbstbiographie*. Leipzig: Brockhaus, 1891.

Spence, Lewis, *The History of Atlantis*. Secaucus, N.J.: University Books, 1968.

Steiger, Brad, *Atlantis Rising*. New York: Dell, 1973.

Wertenbaker, William, *The Floor of the Sea*, Boston: Little, Brown, 1974.

Wunderlich, Hans Georg, *The Secret of Crete*. London: Souvenir Press, 1976.